A LESSON FROM THE SCHOOL
OF HARD KNOCKS

"How old are you again?" Samantha playfully asked.

"Sixteen," I replied with pride.

"Damn, just a baby. Well, I'm gon' teach yo' ass how to be a sex machine." She paused, seductively biting her full bottom lip. "That's if you want to be my student?"

With a wicked smile, I answered, "This'll be one class I'll never skip. Hell, the semester just started, and I already want extra credit."

Our laughter was interrupted by a knock on the front door. It wasn't a neighborly Can-I-borrow-a-cup-of-sugar? kind of knock, but a Bam!-Bam!-Bam!-Open-up-this-door kind of knock.

"Oh shit, it's Darryl!" she said, jumping out of the bed.

"Who the hell is Darryl?" I asked nervously but not really wanting to know the answer.

Samantha then said three words a playa never wants to hear: "He's my husband."

All the Women I've Loved

A NOVEL

BYRON HARMON

POCKET BOOKS
New York London Toronto Sydney

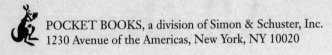
POCKET BOOKS, a division of Simon & Schuster, Inc.
1230 Avenue of the Americas, New York, NY 10020

Library of Congress Cataloging-in-Publication Data

Harmon, Byron.
    All the women I've loved : a novel / Byron Harmon.—1st Pocket
Books trade paperback ed.
      p. cm.
   ISBN 0-7434-8308-1 (trade pbk.)
    1. African American men—Fiction. 2. Washington (D.C.)—Fiction.
3. Journalists—Fiction. I. Title.

PS3608.A748A78 2004
813'.6—dc22

                                   2004044625

First Pocket Books trade paperback edition May 2004

10 9 8 7 6 5 4 3 2 1

For information regarding special discounts for bulk purchases,
please contact Simon & Schuster Special Sales at 1-800-456-6798
or business@simonandschuster.com

Dedicated to my parents,
David and Shirley Harmon

Acknowledgments

I would like to thank God. I am because of You.

I would like to thank my brothers Andre and Marshall. Out of all the things I've done, or ever hope to do, the greatest joy of my life was growing up with you.

I want to thank the Tracy Sherrod Literary Agency. Tracy, Beverly, and Tony. I am blessed to have such a talented and experienced group of people in my corner.

I want to thank my publisher, Louise Burke and my editor, Brigitte Smith. Thanks for your wonderful editorial eye and for believing in this project.

I would like to thank Kimberly Hines, Tia Shabazz, and Carol Mackey. Words cannot properly express how I feel about you ladies and what you've done for me. So I'll keep it simple and say thanks and I love you.

I would like to thank my friends. It's been said that in your darkest hours and when in need of help the only one that you can truly count on is yourself. But every time I've called, you've answered. Every time I've reached out my hand, you've pulled me in, letting me know that even when I couldn't count on myself I could always count on my friends.

I want to thank some brothers who have been down with me from way back. My Army crew: Doug Bennett, Gregory Blue, Eric Devillar, Kenny "KG" Harding, Andre "Dirty Dre" Bowman, and Mike Wilson. "You are all brothers from another mother."

I want to thank my Ill Relatives: Marcus Virgil, Big Ryal, and Drak Muse. "It's our turn now."

I want to thank Kay and Kelly, you read the book when it was on typing paper.

I want to thank Power and Stephanie Leonard. You were there from the beginning. Thanks for everything. I want to thank Corrin Johnson. Your prayers and our long talks were always a source of strength. I want to thank Jennifer Wiggins, Lauren Petterson, Debbie Denmon, Halfreda Anderson, Sunshine, Pamela Crockett, Esq., and Jeffrey Wooten, Esq.

I want to thank my Lake Charles Crew: Dale Arrington. Nelson and Craig Joseph. The late Laron "I bet I can do it" Malbreaux. Harold Guillory and Peter Stewart. I can't forget my brother Roman Thompson.

My Southern University Crew: Craig "CJ Memphis" Johnson, Ms. Campbell, and "Ms. Cleo" Allen.

And I would like to thank Zane, Carl Weber, Eric

Jerome Dickey, E. Lynn Harris, Omar Tyree, and Michael Baisden. Thanks for giving me the blueprint.

A special thanks to Terri McMillan for opening the door. I promise to hold it open for the next generation of writers.

And finally the love of my life Rhadia Hursey and the whole Hursey family.

All the
Women
I've Loved

Chapter One

LeBaron hated wearing a tuxedo. It reminded him of his high school prom. However, as he scanned the ballroom, he couldn't help but think that the White House correspondents' dinner was hardly the prom. It was the biggest broadcasting event of the year. Turnout was always stellar. The air inside the ballroom of Washington, D.C.'s Grand Hilton was electric and thick with the scent of power.

LeBaron and Eric, his best friend, marveled at the dazzling array of personalities in the room.

"There are some rich-ass motherfuckers in here." Eric smiled while sipping on his Rémy and Coke.

"Major players," LeBaron agreed. As he and Eric made their way from the bar, they passed Barbara Walters talking to Tom Brokaw, Alan Greenspan whispering something funny to Chris Rock. It was surreal.

"I can't believe I met Colin Powell," LeBaron said, excitedly elbowing Eric.

"I can't believe how you blew Colin Powell," Eric laughed, making a slurping sound.

"What?"

"Yeah, you was all, 'It's an honor to meet, uh, meet you Mister, I mean, uh, Colonel, General Powell.' You sounded like a lil beeyotch!!"

A skeptical vein creased LeBaron's brow.

"No I didn't."

"Shit, you damn near saluted like you were still in Desert Storm."

"I know you ain't talking? When I introduced you to Soledad O'Brien, you damn near pissed on ya'self."

"She's different."

"How's she different?"

"Soledad O'Brien is way finer than motherfucking Colin Powell."

Laughing, LeBaron looked at his watch. "Damn, we've been gone a minute. We gotta get back to the table."

"No, black man, you gotta get back. I'm here solo. You're the one with wifey."

"Me and Phoenix ain't married."

"Might as well be," Eric said, eyeing a woman in a short, tight black evening dress. "You go on back to Miss Right. I'm 'bout to go holler at Miss Right Now."

LeBaron laughed and gave Eric a pound. As he turned he could hear Eric asking the woman, "Do you believe in love at first sight or should I walk by again?"

* * *

LeBaron spotted Phoenix easily through the crowd, and she waved him over to their table. She looked radiant in her black strapless Donna Karan evening gown, like a cross between Sally Richardson and Halle Berry. LeBaron loved calling her Halle Richardson. As he sat down next to her, he smiled at how lucky he was. He'd recently been promoted to senior executive producer, a title that gave him unquestioned status at his Fox-owned-and-operated TV station. Add to that a pair of news Emmys he'd recently won for Best Newscast and 9/11 coverage, and he felt on top of the world. He had a great career with a bright future. The only thing missing was a wife and kids.

LeBaron couldn't help but think, as he kissed Phoenix on the cheek—much to the delight of his snickering coworkers sitting around the table—that she was definitely "wifey material."

Fox had paid for six tables, but this one was prime. He shared it with Katherine Green, his boss and mentor, along with her date. Next to Katherine was her second in command, Holly Gauntt, and Glenda, Holly's life partner. Across from them were Tracey Neale and Brian Bolter, the station's main anchor team. It was their first introduction to Phoenix, and they peppered her with questions.

"Were they talking your ears off?" LeBaron said, sarcastically scanning the table. Phoenix grinned, then winked. "Oh no, but they are telling me all the office dirt on you."

"What dirt?" LeBaron smirked. "I'm cleaner than the board of health."

Brian saw his opening. "Didn't we just do a story on the city investigating the board of health?" They all laughed.

"LeBaron?" Katherine interrupted. "We're so glad you brought Phoenix out. It's so nice to finally meet her." She turned to Phoenix. "LeBaron is so secretive." The table nodded in agreement.

"Not with me," Phoenix said, rubbing LeBaron's hand. He smiled back at her.

"Aw, they're so cute," Glenda said.

"OK, enough about me," LeBaron said, but Holly cut him off.

"No, LeBaron, you don't get off the hook that easy. When are you and Phoenix tying the knot?"

Oh God, LeBaron thought, a knot slowing tying in his stomach. Suddenly, he felt like he was in a sauna with a fever, eating hot grits and drinking hot chocolate with a mink coat on. Sticking his finger in his collar to loosen it, he managed to stutter an "uh" then turned to Phoenix for help. He got none.

"So?" the table sarcastically said in unison. They looked like a jury, and Phoenix looked like Judge Judy.

"Aren't you going to answer Holly, baby?" she said. It was more of an accusation than a question.

"Well you see what had happened was?" he joked. Nobody got it. Just as the sweat began to pour down LeBaron's forehead, Eric showed up. LeBaron looked at him like he was the United States Cavalry about to save his ass from the Indians.

"What's up?" Eric said, pulling out his chair. Looking at the expectant faces around the table, he said, "Damn, you all look like y'all waiting for the O. J. verdict."

"Close," LeBaron exhaled.

"What are you talking 'bout?"

"Holly just asked me when Phoenix and I are getting married."

Eric scooted his chair up and said matter-of-factly, "Oh, I can tell y'all that."

"Oh really? When?" Tracey said. Eric raised his glass to his lips.

"When Hell freezes over!"

"Eric!" LeBaron kicked his leg.

"Just playing." Eric turned to LeBaron and in his most serious sports anchor voice asked, "So, LeBaron, just when are you and the lovely Phoenix getting married?"

"Well if you all must know, the answer is soon, very soon." He looked at Phoenix. She beamed. It was "breaking news" to her. Raising her glass, Katherine said, "Looks like a toast is in order. Here's to LeBaron and Phoenix, may you both live a long, loving and healthy life."

"To a healthy life!" the table said.

"To a healthy life," LeBaron said, smiling, but he was really thinking of a quick and painless way to end his.

Chapter Two

"Did you really mean what you said?" Phoenix asked as she wiggled her slender hips out of the tight evening dress. It was just after 2 A.M. and she and LeBaron had just returned from the White House correspondents' dinner. After a night of schmoozing and boozing, she was relieved to be back at LeBaron's place. "Damn these heels are killing me— Hello?"

Looking at himself in the bedroom mirror, LeBaron was loosening his tie.

"Huh?"

Just like a man, Phoenix thought. She frowned, then plopped herself down on the couch and began taking off her stockings. "Did you mean it? You know, what you said? 'Bout us getting married soon?"

Jeeesus! Is she drunk? he thought. He hoped. He prayed. LeBaron was still kicking himself for folding under pressure, but hell, they'd had him cornered, what could a brother do?

"I said it, didn't I?"

"That's not what I asked you." Her eyes were like needles pricking at his weak flesh.

He pulled his shirt off, walked over and sat down beside her. He looked her up and down. He thought of how sexy she looked in her matching black satin Victoria's Secret bra and thong set. He then began twirling one of her thick black locks between his fingers. He caressed her cheek. "I bet we're gon have some nice-looking children."

"If they take after their momma," Phoenix giggled.

"How you figure?" He smirked. Although he knew the punch line, he still loved to play along.

Phoenix stood. With one hand, she swept back her long, black hair, then with a straight face said, "Cuz I got Indian in my family."

"Shit." LeBaron shook his head, then reached for the back of her neck, where her hair was the curliest and coarsest. "I've seen yo' broke-ass family, and I'm here to tell you. You might have a few Indians, but you damn sure got a lot of nappy-headed niggas in yo' family too." She laughed, fell back onto his lap and began kissing him.

"I love you."

"I love you too, baby," he said, getting up.

"Where are you going?"

LeBaron walked over to the minibar and began pouring white wine into two crystal glasses. White wine always got

Phoenix horny. Hell, all it took was tap water to get LeBaron horny.

"Boy, you ain't slick. I'm not letting your black ass off that easy. Now answer my question, dammit."

"Damn." He handed her a glass. "I done forgot what the question was."

Her right eye began to arch menacingly.

"Uh-oh," he muttered. "Not the eyebrow?"

"Yes, negro, the eyebrow. Now answer my question or I'm revoking your pussy privileges."

"Since you put it that way," he said as he bear hugged her. "Look here, what did I tell you on our first date?"

When she bit her bottom lip she looked like a sex kitten. "You told me a lot of things silly."

"But what abou—"

"Oh!" She cut him off. "I remember, the poem?"

"What poem?"

The eyebrow arched again. "About the angels?"

"Oh yeah," he followed. "Those angels?"

"Yeah, those angels. Remember now?"

"Of course I do, sweetheart."

Phoenix felt so safe snuggling in his arms. "Recite it to me, LeBaron."

He thought it was so easy to get his woman off track. "I love it when you call me LeBaron. You're lucky I don't have my checkbook handy cuz when you say my name like that I wanna put my—" She put her finger on his lips.

"Shhh," she purred. "The angels?"

"The angels, yeah right?" he agreed.

"You ready?"

"I was born ready." He stood and walked behind her. His lips were less than an inch away from her ears. The white wine and his warm breath bouncing against her earlobes made her insides tingle when he kissed her neck. Phoenix was just getting going.

Then he blew air kisses in her ear. Phoenix was hot and bothered. By the time he licked her neck while gently cupping her breasts from behind, Phoenix damn near came.

"Sweetheart?" he whispered.

"Yes, daddy?" she purred.

> "I was always taught
>   Angels lived High in the Sky
> Floating on Clouds, playing Golden Harps
>   Never to be seen by Human Eyes
>
> But, the first time I saw You
>   I knew that at least one of God's Angels had Left
> To show me the meaning of Beauty and Grace
>   While God kept the rest for Himself"

Phoenix sighed. "That was so beautiful, but I'ma ask yo black ass one mo' gin." She unfastened his belt, then unzipped him and stuck her hand inside his pants. LeBaron was as hard as government cheese.

"Did you really mean what you said at dinner?"

As his pants fell around his ankles, he mumbled, "Of course I did. Of course I . . . oh God!"

Chapter Three

The crown jewel of WTTG FOX5 was its 10 P.M. news-cast, but it was the early morning news that paid the bills. FOX5's *Morning News* was three and a half hours long—great for advertising revenue—but an eternity for a local news station to fill.

The show's popular anchors, along with its balanced mix of news, traffic and weather, kept it atop the ratings in Washington, D.C.'s ultracompetitive market. One of its main attractions was the guest interview segment. Hosted by anchor Robin McCarthy, a dead ringer for Diahne Carroll, the segments never failed to inform, entertain or antagonize. She was a no-nonsense veteran anchor who always managed to book the big, interesting guests, and this morning was no different. Her guest was none other than Dr. Leighton Carter, one of the nation's foremost experts on marriage and relationships.

Dr. Carter had been on shows ranging from *Nightline* to *Oprah*. He was a popular psychiatrist and author of *A Woman's Love*, currently one of the country's hottest relationship books. Dr. Carter was smart, funny and very glib, the type of guest a host could sink her teeth into. He was sometimes called the black Dr. Phil. Women in the newsroom had been buzzing ever since Elisa, the executive producer of planning, had landed the interview.

Many of them had arrived early to meet and have him autograph their book. Normally, newsrooms were louder than a kindergarten class, but everyone was silent as they watched the interview.

"Thanks for joining us, Dr. Carter," Robin began. She looked stunning in a mustard-colored business suit.

"My pleasure," he said, shaking her well-manicured hand. "And please call me Leighton."

"Okay, Leighton. What makes you such an expert on having a good relationship?"

Dr. Carter grinned, flashing a set of perfect thirty-twos. "Robin, I'm not an expert on how to have a good relationship. However, I am known as an expert on how to mess up a good relationship. I just instruct my clients to do the opposite."

"Cute," Robin laughed. "That was real cute."

"And so are you," he deadpanned.

"No, you are not flirting with me on TV?" she shot back.

"It's not flirting when you are stating the obvious."

"Uh uhm," she cleared her throat. "Now let's get back to the book."

LeBaron and Elisa laughed as they watched the interview on the bank of monitors in his office.

"I've never seen anyone get Robin off track like that before," LeBaron said.

"Me either," Elisa agreed. "But you know they used to date?"

"Really?"

"Yeah, long time ago at Georgetown. That's how we got him. He blew off *Good Morning America* to come on with Robin."

"Damn. Former fling or not, he's good, real good."

"Wanna meet him? I'll bring him by your office after the interview."

"Thanks, I'd like that."

"Dr. Leighton Carter," Elisa said, "this is LeBaron Brown, our senior executive producer." Leighton and LeBaron shook hands while she walked back to her cubicle.

"A pleasure and an honor to meet you, Dr. Carter."

"The honor is all mine, and please call me Leighton." His green eyes bored into LeBaron.

"Okay, Leighton," LeBaron said, slightly unnerved. "Please have a seat."

"Thank you." He was so polite, LeBaron thought, but polite in a mad scientist kind of way.

"Dr. Carter—I mean Leighton—I know you don't have much time." LeBaron paused, trying to gather his thoughts.

"I have as much time as I need."

"Well, okay, when is the right time for a man to get married?"

"When the man is ready," Dr. Carter said.

"How do you know when you're ready?"

"If you have to ask, then you're not."

"C'mon, Leighton, you sound like Confucius."

"And you sound confused."

"That's an understatement. You see, I have a girlfriend. Her name is Phoenix and we've been together a few years and I feel like it should be time for us to get married, but I'm not sure." LeBaron waited for him to say something. Dr. Carter was silent. LeBaron continued.

"I feel all this pressure."

"From your girlfriend?" Dr. Carter asked.

"Not so much her as everybody else. You know? Friends. My momma. Wanting a damn grandbaby. Shit, I'm trying to get a babygrand."

"I see," Dr. Carter laughed while stroking his chin with his right hand. He leaned closer and looked right into LeBaron's eyes. "Of course I'd need more time to analyze your situation, but at first glance I'd say that you have all the classic signs of a very common condition." LeBaron was on the edge of his chair.

"Yeah? What is it called?"

Dr. Carter paused and slyly looked over each shoulder for effect.

"It's called 'Scared as Shit.' "

He laughed and stood up to leave.

LeBaron leaned back into his chair and gave him an ah-you-got-me look.

"Seriously, LeBaron. You know when a man is ready to get married?"

"When?" LeBaron asked, standing to shake Dr. Carter's hand.

"When the man no longer asks himself if he's ready."

Chapter Four

Park Avenue in Chevy Chase, Maryland, is a lot like Park Avenue in Manhattan. For one thing, it's hard as hell for a black man to catch a cab and no matter how bright the sun, the area remains in a constant shadow. All along the avenue rich white men and women stream in and out of outrageously expensive boutiques and designer stores. On one corner stands Saks Fifth Avenue and across the street are Brooks Brothers, Cartier, and Gucci. Two blocks down overlooking it all is Tiffany & Co., a tall, light-gray stone monument to a girl's best friend. Not too many brothers frequent this particular store, but on this crisp September afternoon the Vanilla Valhalla of VVS' got a taste of chocolate.

"Fifteen thousand dollars! You're spending fifteen thousand dollars on one woman?" Eric asked while staring at the two-carat princess-cut diamond solitaire nestled inside a platinum band.

Along the counters, salespeople and a few customers whispered and cast furtive glances at the two tall, well-dressed black men staring at the ring under the glass countertop. The guys ignored them; they were used to it, after all. LeBaron frowned at Eric's outburst. He'd asked his future best man to come to Tiffany's for a second opinion, not his personal opinion.

"That's right, one woman," LeBaron said, shaking his head.

"But damn, fifteen thou? Do you know how many women you can buy with fifteen thousand dollars?"

"I don't need many women. I have Phoenix, and she's a perfect ten."

"Shit, with fifteen G's I'd buy three decent-ass fives."

"Eric, your ass would settle for fifteen a'ight ones."

"You know me? Whether they're fat, skinny, tall or bald, I'll bone them all . . . ya'll."

LeBaron motioned Eric to shut up as Mr. Van Dyke, the very formal manager handling his account, walked up.

"Hello, Mr. Brown," he said.

"How are you today, Mr. Van Dyke?"

"Fine, quite fine, sir. Are we ready to make the purchase, sir?"

"We are," interrupted Eric. "Say, uh, Mr. Van Dyke, that's like Dick . . . Van Dyke, right? Fifteen large is kind of steep. Can a brother get a discount?"

"Shut up, Eric," LeBaron said.

"Oh that's quite alright, Mr. Brown." Turning to Eric, Mr. Van Dyke said, "Sorry sir, but Tiffany's doesn't offer, uhm, discounts."

"Pay him no mind, Mr. Van Dyke," LeBaron said. "Here's my credit card."

"Thank you Mr. Brown, I'll be right back."

After Mr. Van Dyke was out of earshot, LeBaron lit into Eric.

"See nigga, you're the reason white people be thinking we're all stupid."

"Be thinking?" Eric shot back. "Where in the hell did you learn how to speak English, in Mexico?"

"You know what I mean." LeBaron said, laughing.

"Man, I don't care 'bout these white folks," Eric frowned. "They damn sho don't care about us."

After paying for the ring with a platinum card, LeBaron, with Eric at his side, strolled out of the store only to be met by a glare from the security guard. The guard, slightly overweight, middle-aged, and very white, was obviously peeved that a black man could afford to shop at Tiffany's. As they walked through the revolving door, Eric couldn't resist a verbal jab. "Hey Sheriff, just think—if you work twenty more years you might be able to afford a ring like my boy here."

Eric was crazy; he'd say anything to anybody, especially women. It was easy for him to charm the ladies; he was, after all, a pretty boy. At six foot two, trim, with smooth brown skin and a smile that made women wet, he was a local celebrity. Sports fans knew him as Eric "2" Swift, a former cornerback with the Washington Redskins until a knee injury ended his three-year career. But Eric had found new stardom on television as a sports anchor for WTTG, the local Fox affiliate, and he milked his fame for all he could. LeBaron and Eric had met at the station eight years before and become fast friends with a lot in common, the most obvious being the fact that they were rare breeds in a city where nearly fifty percent of black men between the ages of seventeen and thirty had been to jail at least once.

The Cheesecake Factory was only a few blocks from Tiffany's, so they decided to go there and grab lunch. LeBaron was fiending for some chicken jambalaya, and the restaurant had some of the best in town. As they exited Tiffany's the two had no idea they were being watched.

The spy walking behind them was Bridgitte Bennett, Phoenix's best friend and coworker. She worked in the accounting department at Saks, and, as luck would have it, she was on her lunch break. Blessed with hawk vision and superior math skills, it took no time for Bridgitte to hone in on the small signature Tiffany's bag. Bridgitte could smell a diamond. As LeBaron and Eric crossed the street, her mind started computing like an IBM mainframe.

"Oh my," she said, smiling, "what do we have here?

LeBaron? Small Tiffany's bag? Large enough to hold at least a two-carat diamond. Anniversary in a few days?" She briefly wondered if she should tell Phoenix or keep the secret. But as anyone who knew her would attest, Bridgitte kept a secret about as well as a police informant.

Chapter Five

"Oh my God!" Phoenix screamed. "Was it really from Tiffany's?"

"I saw the bag and, girl, it was a small bag, too," Bridgitte said.

"How small? Like ring small?"

"It had to be a ring." Bridgitte chattered into her cell phone, oblivious to the people walking along the sidewalk. She didn't even notice the short bald white man coming out of the Bank of America until she walked right into him. "Hello? The word is excuse me!" she snapped, nearly dropping her phone. The man just looked at her nervously and kept on. "Girl, these white people. What was I saying?"

"You were saying that you thought it was a ring."

"Yeah, I mean how long y'all been together?"

"Girl, three long years."

"Then it's 'bout time that negro asked you to marry him."

"I don't—"

Bridgitte cut her off. "Didn't you tell me that lately he's been asking you about kids and stuff?"

"Yeah, the other night at the dinner with his coworkers he said we'd get married soon, but you know men. They're always saying shit just to find out what you're thinking."

"For real, but I know LeBaron is gonna propose, so start looking for that wedding gown."

"Well, I ain't getting my hopes up."

"Then I'll keep mine up for you, at least one of us has hit the man jackpot. Hey, I gotta run, but I'll talk to you later so that we can start planning our—I mean your—wedding."

"Bye, crazy-ass girl, and thanks."

Phoenix's hand trembled as she hung up the phone. She was nervous and happy, shocked and scared.

"Could it be?" she said softly. "LeBaron is gonna ask me to marry him?"

Phoenix had been waiting three years for the day that LeBaron would propose to her. It was the longest relationship she had ever been in. He made her feel so safe. She loved the poems he constantly wrote for her and the little gifts he'd give her. Like the funny *New York Times* newspaper "published" on the date that she was born. The fake headline read "God Blesses the World with Phoenix

Morgan." She felt blessed to have a man like LeBaron. He was everything that she wanted in a man, in a mate. He had education, a promising career, goals, and he was fine as hell. He stood a commanding six foot three inches. The hue of his skin and curly black hair indicated his Creole ancestry. And LeBaron's complexion was such a smooth shade of mocha brown that she knew he'd never had acne as a teenager.

Her mother loved him too. She always asked Phoenix when they were going to get married and give her some pretty grandchildren. Soon she would be able to give her mother a definitive answer.

For thirty minutes Phoenix stared at the mirror on her desk, practicing surprised faces.

"Oh, LeBaron, I've been waiting all my life for this!" She spoke aloud and placed her hands over her heart. "Nah. What about this?" she said. "Oh my God, LeBaron! This ring is so beautiful! Yes, I'll be your bride!" Phoenix rolled her widened eyes and shook her head in dismay. "Nah, I sound like a soap opera actress."

After going through her whole repertoire, Phoenix looked at the photograph on her desk of her and LeBaron in Montego Bay for her last birthday. She closed her eyes and smiled at the memories. She opened her eyes, refocused her attention on her reflection in the mirror, and settled on a simple "Yes, I'll marry you."

* * *

After lunch, LeBaron sat in his office, dreading The Phone Call. The call would be to his mother, Lucille Brown. He knew that she wouldn't like what he had to tell her. Every time he mentioned marrying Phoenix, she'd change the subject. Lucille didn't think he was ready to get married, but then again, she always questioned his decisions. The two had a strained relationship, but she was his mother and he still wanted her approval. While he was his mama's baby, he wasn't a mama's boy. Dante, his older brother, who had a different father, was closer to Lucille. LeBaron worshipped his playboy father, Daniel, a fact not lost on his mother. "You look and act just like yo' no-good-assed daddy," was a phrase LeBaron heard frequently growing up. It usually came after one of Daniel's many indiscretions.

But Lucille kept it real. Even when she'd found out about Daniel's philandering, she hadn't fretted, she'd just cut off the pussy. LeBaron and Dante still cringed when they thought of what she'd told them one night after they had found out their daddy was cheating on her. They'd asked if she was going to divorce him.

"For what?" she'd snorted. "And let some other bitch live in my house. Shiiit! I worked too hard to get this here. Y'all daddy can fuck whoever he wants to, cuz he ain't getting none here, besides his ass got plenty insurance, so when he dies, I'm getting mine."

Sure as hell, when Daniel died, Lucille got nearly three hundred thousand dollars. She was from the old school of motherhood. She whipped the shit out of her kids and would say exactly what was on her mind and didn't give a damn how you felt about it. As LeBaron dialed her number, he knew she was not going to be happy.

"So you bought her the ring, huh?" she said in a tone only she could speak in.

"Um . . . yeah," LeBaron replied. "Uh . . . Momma, I wish you could see it."

LeBaron was glad that he was talking to her on the phone instead of in person, because he didn't have to lie to her face. He imagined where she was sitting. She was probably in the den on one of her overstuffed leather chairs. Daniel had died three years earlier after a heart attack, and since then she had taken up decorating. Every time LeBaron would visit, she'd have the house arranged in a new color.

"Mmm hmm. How much did it cost?"

He paused for what seemed like an hour. "Uh . . . only fifteen thousand dollars," he muttered.

"Fifteen thousand dollars! What? Sweet Holy Jesus! You paid fifteen thousand dollars for a goddam ring? Boy, is you some kind of fool, a stupid fool? You could have given your poor old momma some of that money. Do you know how many bills I could pay with fifteen thousand dollars?"

"Momma, you don't have any bills."

"Shit, I'd find something to pay with that kind of money. That's too damn much money to pay for a ring, LeBaron."

"But I love Phoenix."

"That's all fine and good, son, but how long do you think y'all gon' stay married? Y'all kids today break up on the first date."

LeBaron thought there was no use arguing with her. He wished that his father were alive; he'd understand. He could hear him now. "Son, you only have one life to live and you have to live how you want to."

"Have you seen India lately?" Lucille said, changing the subject.

"Momma, you know I haven't seen her in years."

"Boy, I don't know that. Now that's who you should marry. Y'all made a nice couple."

"She had her chance, but she chose Los Angeles." He frowned.

While his mother didn't dislike Phoenix, she'd always dreamed that someday LeBaron would marry his ex-girlfriend India. He'd once had that same dream, but a nasty breakup had woken him up. They had been together for three years, until one day, without warning, she'd broken up with him and moved to Los Angeles to pursue a legal career. He hadn't seen or heard from her since. It still hurt to think about her.

"Momma, I'm ready to settle down, and Phoenix is the one for me."

"Whatever, boy, I'ma get off this phone, but what you should have done was take some of that money you spent on that ring and saved it."

"Save it for what, Momma?"

"To pay for a divorce."

LeBaron opened his mouth to respond, but the dial tone greeted him on the other end. "Why do I even bother?" he sighed, slamming the phone down.

LeBaron now understood how his father could have died of a heart attack at such an early age. He'd done it to get away from Lucille Brown.

Chapter Six

Zanzibar on the Waterfront, located in front of the Southwest Marina, was one of D.C.'s hottest nightclubs. With two levels offering different types of music, live entertainment, and an upscale restaurant, Zanzibar always drew the biggest crowds. Every Friday night droves of stressed-out young black professionals weary from long days of being young black professionals packed the club to enjoy the free buffet and drink specials. Tonight was no different: The entire building was packed with people, and the various dance floors were home to a decadent display of gyrating, multicolored flesh.

In one room the DJ spun the classic Funkadelic cut "Knee Deep," a guaranteed old-school party starter. Attractive young ladies were coming into the club in sets of five. It was the kind of night Eric lived for.

"Damn," Eric said while making his way through the

crowd of women in tight dresses. "Where's Sisqo? 'Cause tonight the thongs are out in throngs."

"It's too hot and cramped in here," LeBaron yelled back over the loud music. "Feels like the damn *Amistad.*"

"That's fine with me, dog, 'cause tonight I'm partying like a newly freed slave."

After getting their drinks—a Courvoisier and Coke for Eric and a Rémy Martin on the rocks for LeBaron—they made their way into Eric's favorite spot, the VIP room. It made Eric feel like even more of a celebrity. They waved at a few people they knew before settling down in the back next to a table occupied by a set of attractive twins. The women smiled at them, and Eric winked back. One of the benefits of the VIP room was that it weeded out all the broke and ugly people. So you knew that whomever you talked to had a good job, a hefty bank account, or was at least good-looking.

"Yo, I think you're making a big mistake," Eric said while sipping his drink. "Why do you want to get married when you can have damn near any of these women in here?"

"E, chasing these kind of women is played out. All they want is a nigga with phat money and a phat car, but all they're bringing to the table is a phat ass."

"Hell, that sounds like an even trade to me," Eric said, shaking his head. "I guess Phoenix didn't want any of that from you?"

"That's different, we have a relationship."

"Y'all ain't always had a relationship. You know Phoenix's snobby ass wouldn't have even looked at you sideways if you weren't a good-looking, six-figga nigga."

"Whatever, she makes me happy. Shit, she's paid too. It ain't like I'm supporting her."

"All I'm saying is this—look at you, man, cats dream about our lives. I ain't gay or nothing, but you're handsome, not as pretty as Muhammad Ali or me but handsome nevertheless. You're thirty-two years old, got a big-assed Lexus, and a phat town house. That's the shit young niggas dream about and why we worked so hard to get it. And now that you finally got it you want to punk out and turn in your playa card? Fuck that, getting married is like joining the Witness Protection Program. It's the beginning of an unfamiliar new life with an unfamiliar new name: husband. And, bruh, I'm too selfish to be selfless."

LeBaron hated when Eric would go off player philosophizing—partly because it had a ring of truth to it. It was scary; sometimes he felt like Eric was the devil showing him all the things he could have if he would just sell his soul.

"Eric, there's more to life than chasing women."

"I know, but nowadays marriage ain't what it used to be. Fifty percent of them fail. Then you got to pay all that fucking alimony and child support. It ain't worth it when you can just rent the pussy. And riddle me this, Batman? How many of our boys are married?"

LeBaron thought for a moment.

"About five."

"Now answer me this, how many of them have told us at one time or another they hated being married?"

LeBaron didn't answer because they both knew. All of them hated being married.

"See, it's all good when you first get married, great sex and home cooking. Every day it's pussy and pancakes. But then after a while that shit gets old. She won't want to have that wild and freaky sex no more, and that's when y'all gon' start arguing all the fucking time and then your ass ends up jacking off and eating TV dinners every night. Besides, Phoenix's ass can't even cook anyway."

"Whatever," LeBaron said, laughing. "You're just fucked up, that's all. Some woman must have really done a number on yo' ass, 'cause you sound like one bitter-ass motherfucker. Keep that up and your ass is going to be that brother Chris Rock talked about, the old single man in the club." Eric laughed so hard he nearly spit out his drink.

"Well, watch this old ass man operate in the club." Eric leaned over and introduced himself to one of the twins at the next table.

"Excuse me, miss, are you from Tennessee?"

"No," she said, slightly confused. "Why do you ask?"

Eric grinned and said, "Because you're the only Ten up in here that I see."

She was getting ready to blow him off like she had every other guy who'd approached her wrong tonight, but she stopped herself when she looked at Eric's face. "I know you. You're on TV, right?"

Eric shook his head. "Who, me? Nah, I'm a chiropractor."

"No, you aren't," the other twin leaned forward and spoke up. "What's your name?"

"My patients call me Dr. Back Cracker." They all laughed, including LeBaron. He thought briefly about how much he was going to miss hanging out like this.

Tasha and Tanya Thompson were beautiful twins who'd once modeled for Wrigley's Doublemint chewing gum when they were younger. But now that they had grown up, they absolutely hated to be reminded of it. It had been five years since their commercials had aired, but guys still came up to them saying, "I'd like to double my pleasure." Nowadays the twins modeled for department store catalogs and moonlighted as Redskins cheerleaders. They had all been talking for half an hour when LeBaron's pager vibrated. He didn't have to look at it. He knew it was Phoenix wondering where he was. He was ready to leave anyway as he reached for his jacket.

"Where you going, handsome?" Tasha asked, tugging gently on his arm.

LeBaron looked at her plunging neckline and rising hem as she crossed her legs. *Damn, we could really mingle if I was single*, he thought.

Eric, who was buzzing off the cognac, cut him off

before he could answer. "Oh, he's about to get engaged tomorrow, and he's got to go check in with wifey."

Tasha frowned at the thought of such a good prospect being taken off the market. It was the same old story—the men she was interested in were either gay, bi-sexual or already involved in a relationship. A few more nights like this and she was going to start dating white men.

"And guess how much this nigga paid for the engagement ring?" Eric blurted out.

The twins were real curious now and turned their heads to look at LeBaron, who was eyeing Eric hard. "Fifteen fucking thousand dollars, can you believe that shit?"

On cue the twins blurted out, "Fifteen thousand dollars? You spent fifteen thousand dollars on a ring?"

Sometimes LeBaron wondered why he ever hung out with Eric. He could be such a pain in the ass.

"Why don't y'all ask Eric what he got on his last AIDS test?" LeBaron cracked, turning the focus away from him.

They turned and stared at Eric.

Without missing a beat he shot back, "Passed it, got a sixty-five."

The twins laughed uneasily. LeBaron grinned while putting his jacket on.

"Nice meeting you, ladies. And, asshole, do you want me to drive your drunk ass home?"

Eric put his arms around the twins and said, "Nah,

family man, I'm in good hands with the Doublemint Girls."

The twins looked at each other, rolled their eyes and got up, leaving Eric at the table laughing at his joke and LeBaron laughing at Eric.

Chapter Seven

After taking a very drunk Eric home, LeBaron fell into deep thought as he drove to Phoenix's house. He kept hearing his mother's warnings and Eric's lecture. He was starting to get confused and have doubts. So he did what he always did when those thoughts crept in: He thought about Phoenix.

Phoenix Morgan had come out of nowhere, clouding his mind with thoughts of love and hope. Ironically, they'd met at a wedding. Mimi Dunham, a distant cousin of his, was getting married, and Phoenix had been one of her bridesmaids. LeBaron's mother had been the one invited to the wedding, but she'd had the flu and had sent him in her place. He hated weddings, and it was definitely not how he'd wanted to spend his Saturday afternoon. LeBaron barely knew Mimi and hadn't seen her since they were in elementary school. His mother had pleaded with him that someone from the family had to be there. LeBaron had acquiesced and had even arrived on time for the ceremony.

The wedding had been held at Metropolitan Baptist, one of Washington, D.C.'s oldest and most historic black churches. LeBaron had been impressed at how beautifully the church had been prepared. The pews had been draped in white silk trimmed with gold ribbon. The sanctuary had smelled of roses, lilac and jasmine.

After the last guests had been seated, a soloist had begun to softly sing Stevie Wonder's "Ribbon in the Sky." An adorable flower girl, who couldn't have been any more than four, had walked up the aisle dropping tiny handfuls of rose petals in her wake. Next had come the twelve brides-maids. They had been so gorgeous that any one of them could have been a bride. LeBaron had made a vow right then to keep in touch with "Cousin" Mimi.

Phoenix had been the last to walk down the aisle, and when LeBaron had seen her he'd understood how Adam must have felt when he'd first seen Eve. She'd been daz-zling in her gold silk shantung gown. Phoenix's skin was café au lait. Her eyes had shone like black diamonds, and her long, dark hair had bounced about her shoulders. LeBaron had been enchanted and hypnotized by her confi-dent walk.

Their eyes had met for a brief moment. Her lips had pursed into a beautiful smile. His jaw had dropped.

After the ceremony was over, LeBaron had introduced

himself and they'd become fast friends. Four months later, they were a couple. The two would speak on the phone for hours at a time and frequently met for lunch or late-night trips to Starbucks. Phoenix was the first woman that LeBaron ever went on vacation with. She was a lot of firsts for him. Most importantly, Phoenix was the first woman whose mind impressed him. It was easy to think of her as "wife material." The copies of bridal magazines on her coffee table helped too. LeBaron felt a little pressure and was wary of giving up his freedom, but deep down he knew that he could never find another woman like her.

Phoenix was twenty-seven years old, intelligent, beautiful, and made nearly as much money as he did as an assistant buyer for Saks Fifth Avenue. She was so successful that she had been picked to go on her first buying trip to Fashion Week in Paris, where the upcoming spring ready-to-wear shows were being held. Her Lufthansa flight was scheduled to leave Sunday, the day after their anniversary dinner. It was quite an accomplishment for someone her age to be invited. Saks had a reputation for favoring older, whiter women for the perks-filled trip. LeBaron was proud of her, but he wasn't excited that the trip was for two weeks. In their entire relationship, they hadn't been apart for more than a week. He had thought about taking a vacation and going with her, but Phoenix had squashed that idea. The trip was too important for her career to add the distraction of bringing her man along. Pulling his car into her driveway, he thought about asking her again.

Phoenix lived in a quiet suburb in Laurel, Maryland, in a three-story burnt orange brick town house. As LeBaron walked up the driveway, he could see her peeking through the curtain. When she opened the door, he was speechless.

The living room was dimly lit with candles, and the aroma of incense filled the air. "If Only for One Night" by Luther Vandross played softly in the background. Phoenix looked delicious as the candlelight silhouetted her sexy curves. She wore a thigh-length short red silk robe that she had picked up earlier at Victoria's Secret, but it hid none of hers. As LeBaron closed the door and walked in, she loosened her belt and let the robe fall to the floor. She was naked, her body glistening from Sweet Temptations perfumed lotion. He thought he was either drunk or dreaming. He had never seen her like this before, but he loved it.

"Baby, what's all this for?"

Phoenix didn't answer. Instead, she unbuttoned his shirt and gently ran her hands across his chest and began kissing his neck. LeBaron tensed up, closed his eyes, and moaned. He tried to hold her, but she pushed him away.

"Ohh, Phoenix . . . baby . . . what's gotten into you?"

She ignored him. Her hands moved from his chest to his waist. She unbuckled his belt, unzipped his slacks and slipped her hand inside. "Nothing's gotten into me . . . yet," she finally answered. "But I'm hoping that something will soon."

LeBaron couldn't hold back any longer. He lifted

Phoenix in his arms and carried her to the couch. "Lay on your stomach and close your eyes," he said. Phoenix obeyed, and he began gently massaging her shoulders.

"Mmm," Phoenix moaned. "A little lower, please." He moved his hands further down her back. "Yeah, right there, Daddy." He loved it when she called him Daddy. He blew softly in her ear, taking time to suck and nibble on her lobe. He kissed her neck, then slowly trailed kisses down her spine, stopping just long enough to lick the small of her back and squeeze her ass. LeBaron then got down on both knees and kissed her lower and lower.

Phoenix strained to keep still. "Oh shit, I can't take that, baby."

"Oh, you gon' take it, and you gon' like it."

"Yes . . . Daddy." She squirmed back into the cushion. LeBaron kissed her thighs, calves and, finally, her toes. "Oh shit . . . not the toes."

He slowly raised her foot, put the big toe in his mouth and sucked it like a pacifier. "Oh God," Phoenix screamed.

LeBaron inched his fingers up her leg, finding their destination between her thighs. She began biting the cushion of the couch. "You like that, huh?"

"Oh . . . shit . . . damn . . . I do."

"Tell me then."

"Oh . . . baby . . . I love it when you . . . ah . . . ohh . . ." Phoenix felt as if she was losing her mind as LeBaron stroked her with his hand.

"Anybody ever made you feel like this before?"

"No." Deep inside her heart and other places she knew she was telling the truth.

"Turn over." Once again she obeyed. She spread her legs as wide as possible, setting one on the floor and the other over the back of the couch. Looking down, LeBaron knew why babies waited so long to come out. Hell, he wanted to go back in. He licked her navel and began the slow descent. "Phoenix, I think you should know something."

"What is it?"

"I haven't eaten all day."

"Well, *bon appétit.*"

Phoenix came over and over again, the waves of pleasure rolling over her body, shaking her down to her bones. Once she regained her composure, she purred, "Now it's my turn, Daddy. Lie back."

LeBaron obeyed, and they switched places. Piece by piece, she pulled off his shoes, slacks and silk boxers. "Damn," she said. "Aren't we excited? I want you to close your eyes."

"Okay."

"Now shut up. You are not allowed to talk until I say so. Understand?"

"Yes."

"I thought I told you to shut up?"

He nodded his head.

"Get up." She helped him to his feet and led him over to the chair. "Now sit down." LeBaron reached behind him for balance and sat down. The chair was cold for a few seconds before he got comfortable.

Phoenix stood behind him, her soft round breasts pressed against his shoulders. She slowly worked her fingers into his thick curls and blew softly in his ear. "You like that, baby?" He nodded. She grabbed a handful of hair and gently pulled back his head. She arched his neck and nibbled, then rubbed an ice cube where she'd nibbled. LeBaron jumped from the cold. After a few minutes of kissing and nibbling, she stopped and stepped back. Puzzled, he turned his head to get a sense of where she was going. Phoenix slowly walked around him just out of his reach. She stopped in front of him and knelt between his legs. Pressing her body close, she ran her fingers over his chest, stomach, pelvis and thighs. He reached for her. "Put your hands down," she said while pushing his arms away. She then put another ice cube inside her mouth. She kissed his chest, and he squirmed. She sucked one of his nipples, and he sighed. Her cool lips and tongue tested his tolerance level as she methodically kissed and licked his stomach.

"You like this?"

He moaned. She licked lower, to his navel.

"What about this?"

He tried to moan, but the sound wouldn't form. He was too dizzy with pleasure and anticipation. Phoenix crunched the ice in her mouth and kept kissing and licking him lower and lower. "God, that feels so good," LeBaron mumbled. His eyes rolled back in ecstasy. He felt like a giant Tootsie

Roll. He was about to explode when Phoenix stopped. She stood up and put her hands on his shoulders. Straddling LeBaron, she gently lowered herself down onto him.

"You can talk now," she whispered.

LeBaron wrapped his arms around Phoenix and squeezed her body close to his. "I love you, Phoenix Morgan."

LeBaron smiled as he listened to the soft sounds of Phoenix sleeping. He loved the way she purred like a kitten after making love. He also loved her room. Her cherry-wood sleigh bed was enormous. It was a graduation present from her grandmother, and it took up almost the entire bedroom. On her walls hung different-shaped mirrors and lithographs by black artists.

There were teddy bears in every corner, as if standing guard. She'd had them for years, many of them gifts from past boyfriends. LeBaron hated them and joked that one day he was going to bear-nap them and throw them away.

Man, Phoenix was out of control. He was worn out, and, judging by the way her leg hung off the bed, she must have been too. She was amazing. *Will it be like this when we get married? According to Eric, probably not.* Looking at the gentle rise and fall of her breasts, he wished he could sleep as soundly, but at the moment his mind was spinning. Last night had been icing on the wedding cake, but he couldn't shake the fear eating away at him. He wondered if his mother and Eric were right about marriage. Hell, after all, he was only thirty and just starting to enjoy his success. Why give up his freedom so soon? And what about all his friends who were married and miserable? LeBaron believed in odds, and the odds were stacked against him. *But God*, he thought, *she looks so beautiful lying there*. What man wouldn't love waking up to someone as beautiful as her every morning? He cuddled closer, kissed her cheek and softly said, "What am I going to do, baby?"

"Huh?" Phoenix mumbled. LeBaron didn't know if she was awake or just talking in her sleep.

"Uh . . . I said, 'What am I going to do with you?' "

Groggily, she giggled, "Aw . . . I . . . love you, too."

LeBaron shook his head and smiled. He closed his eyes and drifted off into an uneasy sleep.

Chapter Eight

LeBaron yawned and tried to rub the sleep out of his eyes. He rolled over and reached for Phoenix, but the sheets on her side of the bed were cool. He propped himself up on his elbows and noticed that there was a Post-it note attached to the face of the digital clock on the nightstand.

Good morning, sweetheart. I've gone to the hairdresser to get beautiful. See you tonight. Love always, Phoenix.

"Love always . . . always," LeBaron said to himself as he crumpled the note. He exhaled deeply and looked back at the clock, which read 11 A.M. "Oh shit. The Afro-Hut is gon' be packed." LeBaron made his way to the bathroom to get ready for his trip to the barbershop to get "fly."

* * *

Phoenix eased into the stylist's chair.

"How you want it today?" LaTanga asked in between smacks of her gum.

"Girl," Phoenix said looking in the wall mirror, "I want an updo, something that will look right with an evening dress."

"Evening dress? What's the occasion?"

"It's my three-year anniversary."

Heads in wraps, rollers and braids turned her way, interested. Even a few under the dryers looked up.

"You and LeBaron been together three years?"

"Yeah, amazing, huh?"

"That's all right, girl, shit! He got a brother? 'Cause I'm tired of these useless men 'round here." There was a chorus of "Ain't that the truth" and "Amen, sista" from women sitting around the shop.

LaTanga Hamilton was one of the best beauticians in the District and one of the loudest. Every day except Sundays, Mondays, and holidays she held court, dispensing feminist wisdom at her salon, A Cut Above, on Georgia Avenue. The main topics were hair and black men, and LaTanga could talk about both all day. "I'm excited for you, girl," she said, then deadpanned, "at least somebody is happy. Me and my boyfriend broke up on our last anniversary." The listening ladies roared with laughter.

"I'm sorry to hear that, girl, but I think LeBaron's gon' propose tonight."

"Propose? How you figure?"

"Well, we've been dating three years. That's a long time, you know."

"That don't mean nothing," said Brenda, a forty-year-old full-figured woman sitting in the chair next to Phoenix. "Me and my man Earl been going together for ten years and he ain't asked me to marry him yet."

"I don't blame him, 'cause your ass is stupid," LaTanga jumped in. "I ain't dating no nigga for ten years. What's he waiting on? He trying to save up his Social Security checks to pay for the wedding?"

"You ain't even funny," Brenda replied through pursed lips.

"But I do got a point tho'. Don't go counting your chickens before you make the red beans." The ladies shook their heads. LaTanga was notorious for mixing sayings. Frowning, she said, "Y'all bitches know what the hell I mean."

"Well," Phoenix said, "my friend Bridgitte saw him coming out of Tiffany's with a bag—a real small bag." The ladies turned to look at LaTanga.

"He could have had some really small earrings in that small box." Now the ladies, laughing once again, turned to look at Phoenix, like fans at a tennis match.

"Nah, I know it's a ring, he gave me earrings earlier this year for my birthday."

"OK, if you say so, but LaTanga ain't believing a damn thing until she sees a ring."

"And that's why you're alone." Phoenix's reply was followed by hoots and hollers.

"Now what kinda style did you say you want?" La Tanga said, twirling a pair of scissors on her index finger. "A mohawk?"

"I ain't lying, son," Rahiem said, slowly edging the head of a young brother sporting cornrows. "Her room was so small, I stretched out on her bed and my feet were on her dresser."

The barbershop erupted in laughter and a chorus of "You crazy."

"That ain't all either. Her bathtub was so dirty I had to take a shower with my shoes on." More laughter.

For black men, barbershops were like group therapy sessions. There was always a heated discussion going on, and freethinking was not only encouraged but also expected. The daily debates at the Afro-Hut were usually moderated by Rahiem, the most popular and funniest barber. He kept everybody laughing. As usual, on a Saturday morning, the shop was packed. Four barbers worked, but there was always at least a forty-five-minute wait. All types flocked to the small barbershop on Fayette Street in downtown Baltimore. An off-duty cop could be sitting next to a thugged-out drug dealer and it was all good. The scene was don't-ask-don't-tell in its purest sense. Customers certainly didn't come for the décor, because the Afro-Hut was a dump. On the dingy walls were pictures of out-of-fashion hairstyles from the seventies, along with a decade worth of *Jet*'s Beauty of the Week clippings. On the stereo a steady stream of oldies played. The Afro-Hut kept it real—real ghetto. The customers came to the spot because the barbers were the best. They routinely took first place at local and regional hair shows. Two years ago at a competition in New York, Rahiem was named Barber of the Year, although he proclaimed himself Most Valuable Playa.

LeBaron was making his way to an empty chair when Rahiem said, "What up, LeBaron?"

LeBaron braced himself, because when Rahiem said your name he was usually about to bust on you. "Nothing much, what's up with you?"

"I'm chilling, but I got a question. Why in the hell did yo' parents name you after a car, and a wack-ass car at that?" Suddenly the barbershop was like *Showtime at the Apollo*. High fives and "oohs" could be heard all around.

LeBaron shook his head in surrender. "I don't know, dude, they just did."

"I'm saying, if they was gon' name you after a car at least it should've been some fly shit like Cadillac or Bentley." More laughter.

"A'ight, you got me."

"You know I'm just trippin', but where's that fine-ass girlfriend you got? What's her name, Felix?" Another round of laughter erupted.

"It's Phoenix, not Felix. You gotta be one of the dumbest Muslims in the Nation of Islam. I wonder if Farrakhan knows about you?"

"Man, fuck them nasty-ass bean pies. I ain't in that shit. I am a real Mus—"

"Bullshit," LeBaron cut him off. "I picked you up a ham sandwich last week." More laughter, only this time they were laughing at Rahiem.

"Anyway, bruh, where's yo' girl at?" Looking around the room, Rahiem said, "Y'all got to see this muh-fucka's girl, look just like Sally Richardson."

"She's at the beauty shop. By the way, where's yo' momma?"

"Now why you got to talk about my momma? You know my momma dead."

A young brother in the back yelled out, "She ain't dead, she's the living dead, sucking on that crack pipe."

"Fuck you, Tariq," Rahiem snapped. "Yo' momma in jail so yo' ass needs to chill. Now back to you," Rahiem addressed LeBaron. "She's at the beauty shop, and you're at the barbershop. Where the fuck y'all going tonight, the prom?"

"Nah man, it's our three-year anniversary." As soon as he said it, LeBaron wished that he hadn't.

"Damn, three years with the same woman? I bet you done forgot how to fuck." Customers turned to nudge each other, while others were falling over each other laughing.

"Shut up, Rahiem. You should be following that brother's example, instead of trickin' yo' dough on them chickenheads." It was André, one of the other barbers and the elder statesman of the shop. Where Rahiem was crazy, André was logical.

"Thank you, Dré," LeBaron said, "finally a voice of reason."

"Man, fuck that, three years is too damn long to be with one woman," Rahiem said. "Y'all engaged?"

LeBaron was wishing that he wasn't having this conversation. "I'ma ask her tonight."

"No shit, son," yelled Sean, the third and youngest of the barbers. Sean was one of those light-skinned, pretty niggas and was definitely anti-marriage. "Potna', I'm with Rah on this one. I don't trust a bitch for shit. I done ran up in too many married ho's to fall for that marriage shit."

"You're just young," André said. "When you get older you'll understand that when you find the right one, or if she finds you, marriage can be a beautiful thang."

"Whatever's clever," Sean said, winking. "But I done met some old wives who had some old-ass husbands, and they still fucked me."

"I'm telling you," Rahiem jumped in, "getting married is like joining the army, so just get ready to say good-bye to your old life and friends 'cause it ain't coming back."

André jumped back in. "See, it's niggas like you who fuck it up for all the good brothers."

"So," Rahiem kept on, "y'all so-called good brothers are going to eventually fuck it up too."

"Whatever, just cut my hair," LeBaron said while sitting in Rahiem's chair. "I came here for a haircut, not a sermon."

The Saturday afternoon traffic on the Baltimore-Washington Parkway resembled rush hour on a Monday morning. What was normally a thirty-minute drive was taking LeBaron more than an hour—just enough time for him to get lost in his thoughts. *Damn, I'm making a big mistake*, he thought. *I ain't ready to get married. Marriage? I must be crazy, that shit Eric was saying is so true, even them dumb-ass niggas at the barbershop was making some sense. Shit, all my boys who are married hate it, and what if Phoenix turns out like my mother. Daddy said momma was the sweetest woman he had ever met.* "Fuck it, fuck it, fuck it." LeBaron looked at his watch. "Damn, it's three o'clock." He had to hurry home to get dressed so that he could pick Phoenix up by six. But before he could go home, he had one more important stop to make. Passing up his exit, he instead got on the I-495 Beltway.

I hope it's not too late, he thought.

Phoenix looked at her reflection and started stressing out. "Does this dress make me look fat?" she said while sucking in her already flat stomach and turning sideways in the full-length mirror to once again look over the dark navy blue evening dress with matching high heels and a black pearl necklace.

It was LeBaron's favorite outfit. He had picked out each piece and bought it for her to wear to last year's Christmas party at the TV station.

"Hello, you're not listening to me. Bridgitte, does this dress make me look fat? Well, what do you think? I look like a pig, huh?"

Bridgitte put the copy of *Essence* on the nightstand and rolled her eyes. "Girl, you are buggin' out. How in the hell can a dress make you look fat when you don't have any fat?"

Ignoring the comment, Phoenix mumbled, "Ugh, I hate the way I look in this dress. Maybe I should tell LeBaron that we could just stay here and watch TV? I could even cook a candlelight dinner."

Bridgitte laughed as she reached for one of the over-stuffed pillows on the bed. Folding it in her arms, she said, "Shit, the only thing you can cook is grits, and a plate of grits and BET doesn't sound too romantic, even if they are cheese grits."

"Will you shut up!" Phoenix folded her arms across her chest in mock disgust and pouted. "You're supposed to be my best friend."

"I am, and that's why I'm saying you are trippin'. Phoenix, you look fantastic, and your hair is perfect. LeBaron is going to pass out when he sees how beautiful you look."

"You really think so?"

"Would I lie to you?"

Phoenix raised her left eyebrow.

"Let me rephrase that. Would I lie to you about something as important as this? And on your engagement night too?"

"Thanks, girl. I love you," Phoenix said as she walked over to hug her.

"I better leave now before LeBaron gets here and I start crying. Now don't forget to call me as soon as he pops the question, OK?"

"Got it."

Before she walked out the door, Bridgitte turned around and hugged Phoenix again. "I'm so happy for you."

"Thanks, if it wasn't for you I wouldn't have any idea about the ring."

Bridgitte smiled broadly. "What's the use of having a best friend if she can't tell you stuff that your boyfriend wouldn't want you to know?"

Chapter Nine

Sinking into the plush leather seats of the limousine, LeBaron couldn't help but reflect on how far he'd come. He was doing OK for a poor country boy from the small town of Lake Charles, Louisiana.

"Yeah," he said, pouring himself a Rémy Martin and looking around the luxurious limo, "I could get used to this shit."

LeBaron's cell phone jolted him. "Hello?" he said, nearly spilling his drink.

"Where are you?"

"I'm turning into your driveway."

"No you're not. I'm looking out the window now, and I don't see your— Wait, are you in that? Oh shit, is that a limo?"

"Yep, nothing but the best for the best."

"Oh my God! I'll be right down." Phoenix hung up the

phone, screamed, picked it back up, and speed-dialed Bridgitte.

"Hello," Bridgitte said.

"Girl, LeBaron's outside in a limo."

"Stop lying."

"I'm not. Oh my goodness, I think he really is gonna propose."

"And? That's what you wanted, right?"

"Yeah, but it's so—"

"Hey," Bridgitte cut her off, "quit talking to me and go get in the damn limo."

"OK, I'll call you later."

LeBaron stood outside talking with Ali, the chauffeur. "What's taking this woman so long? I bet she's on the phone with her friend Bridgitte telling her about the limo."

"Yeah," Ali said, "American women get much excited about riding in such nice cars."

"I guess the women don't in Saudi Arabia, huh? Y'all probably make them run behind the car."

"No, sir," Ali said, "we've become quite tolerant of the weaker sex, now we let them ride in the trunk."

The squeaking of Phoenix's front door interrupted their laughter. She locked the door and strode to the limo. "Damn," they both said in unison, one with a Southern drawl, the other with an Arabic lilt.

"My eyes never seen such beautiful woman as she, up close like dis."

"Me either," a dazed LeBaron mumbled, barely understanding what in the hell Ali had just said. Phoenix saw their reaction, and a confident grace dominated her steps. It seemed to take her an eternity to walk to the car, and LeBaron enjoyed every second. Ali was stunned and sweating her hard.

"Excuse me, miss, but you look—"

"Slow your roll," LeBaron interrupted. "You got to get your own, my Arabian brother." Turning to Phoenix, he said, "Sweetheart, you look magnificent."

"Thanks, you look quite handsome yourself."

"Yes, he does, does not he?" Ali grinned. LeBaron gave him an evil look, and Ali quickly opened their door and ushered them into the limo.

"Ali," LeBaron said while buzzing the intercom, "put in that CD I gave you."

"Yes, sir." A few seconds later, the smooth sounds of Maxwell wafted through the speakers.

"Oh goody!" Phoenix squealed. "My favorite!"

"You like Maxwell, huh?"

Lip-syncing to "Lifetime," she said, "You know I love him."

"More than me?"

"Not in that way, silly; I love his music."

"Mmm hmm, you better."

"I heard he's in town this weekend and tickets were sold

out months ago." Phoenix sighed and pouted her glossy lips.

"Hey, Ali?" LeBaron buzzed again.

"Yes, sir?"

"Take us to the Maxwell concert."

"No problem, sir."

LeBaron kicked his feet up and reclined into the seat. He nonchalantly looked at Phoenix, who was about to burst.

"Huh? You mean we're going to see Maxwell tonight?"

"Yes, he's at Constitution Hall."

"Ahh!" Phoenix screamed. "Oh God, I love you!"

"Look at what a brotha's gotta do to get his woman to say she loves him."

As the limo got on the Parkway heading toward D.C., Phoenix snuggled close to LeBaron and kissed him on the cheek. "Baby, you're the best," she whispered into his ear.

"The best? Shit, I better be the only."

A Maxwell concert was always a hot ticket in D.C., so the scene inside and outside Constitution Hall was electric. At least a hundred unlucky fans hoping to pick up a late ticket crowded each entrance, and scalpers were trying to make last-minute deals.

As the limo pulled in a crowd of fans moved toward the car, hoping to get a glimpse of its occupants. "Oh my God, they must think we're celebrities," Phoenix said.

"Well," LeBaron said, "tonight you are."

"Quit playing, LeBaron. I'm not getting out of this car, tell the driver to drop us off up the street."

"Up the street? You don't get out of a limo up the damn street." After a few minutes of waiting for Ali to get out, LeBaron buzzed the intercom. "Ali?"

"Yes, sir?"

"Damn, can you get out and open the door?"

"Yes, sir, oh so sorry, my bad."

Turning to Phoenix, LeBaron whispered, " 'My bad'? Ali is fucking up his tip."

Phoenix didn't hear him because she was too busy looking at the growing crowd outside the window. "I'm not getting out of the car."

"Well, I guess one of these hot young thangs'll take your place in the front row—"

"What? You got us row front, I mean, damn I can't even talk. You got us front row seats?"

"That's right, you know how I roll."

"Shoot, what we waiting on?" Phoenix said, moving toward the door. "Let's meet our public."

Ali held the door open while LeBaron stepped out holding Phoenix's hand. The crowd went from anticipation to a confused look that said, Yeah y'all two look fly as hell, but who in the hell are you?

Phoenix got out of the limo as if the crowd wasn't even there. Turning to LeBaron, she said, "Baby, I could get used to this."

"Me too, me too." LeBaron escorted Phoenix up the

stairs to an entrance of the historic Constitution Hall. Once inside the building, an usher brought them down the center aisle of the hall to their coveted seats.

"LeBaron, I'm so excited about tonight. I can't believe you did this for me. Thank you," Phoenix gushed.

"I should be thanking you for being with me."

"I'm the lucky one, sweetheart, but I have a question."

"Shoot."

"It's something that I've been wondering about for a while."

"Yeah, and?" LeBaron said, not really knowing where she was going with this.

"Uh, well, I wanted to know, what did you get me?"

"Get you? What are you talking about?"

"My anniversary present, silly."

"This is it."

"Excuse me?" Phoenix looked mildly insulted.

"Sike! Don't worry about that, you'll find out soon enough."

"Please, I've been dying to know."

"Keep breathing a little longer."

"Pretty please?" She batted her eyelids.

"If you must know, I got you a—" LeBaron stopped in midsentence as the lights dimmed and people started hollering and clapping.

"Okay, shh," Phoenix said putting her finger to her lips. "Tell me later."

The heavy burgundy curtain parted, and the crowd

responded with deafening applause. The funky bass line from his hit "Sumthin' Sumthin' " thumped, and Maxwell emerged from a raised platform. The crowd rose to its feet and Phoenix was out of her seat, shaking what her momma gave her and singing along. Oblivious to Maxwell, LeBaron smiled as his eyes followed Phoenix's gyrations.

"D.C., can I do a li'l sumthin' sumthin' with you?" Maxwell flirted with the already captivated audience. He smoothly segued into the bulk of his repertoire. Ladies swooned and playas took notes as Maxwell mesmerized everyone with his music. At the midpoint of the show Maxwell brought out a stool and sat down. A steady stream of women made their way to the stage to bestow various gifts on Maxwell. After ten minutes of accepting tokens of his fans' affection, Maxwell repositioned himself on the stool and talked to the audience. "You know, D.C., I owe a large part of my success to you. Without you I'd still be eating Cap'n Crunch for every meal and washing dishes in the Village."

"You'd be one fine-ass dishwasher!" a woman in the audience hollered.

Maxwell smiled humbly as the crowd roared. "Seriously, you know what I love more than the money and the fame? It's helping couples to fall in love."

"You got that baby-making music, honey," someone else in the crowd yelled.

"I hope y'all are married, though," Maxwell fired right back.

"Marry me, Maxwell!" another young lady screamed.

Maxwell laughed with the audience. "Yesterday morning I was interviewed on Fox Morning News. Y'all know the local morning show with Robin McCarthy. Well, I met a cool, decent brotha there. His name's LeBaron, and he's the senior executive producer. He told me that his lady, Phoenix, was a big fan of mine." Maxwell got off the stool and stood right in front of Phoenix. He bent down on one knee to get a closer look at her. Phoenix looked from Maxwell to LeBaron with tears in her eyes, a combination of love and embarrassment on her face. "Well, after seeing how beautiful you are, Phoenix, let me say that I'm a big fan of yours." She put her face in her hands while LeBaron held her. "Oh, Phoenix, LeBaron said something else to me. He said that he's so fortunate to have you in his life." Maxwell began singing one of his more popular songs, "Fortunate." The crowd sang every word. When he finished, every woman in the audience was crying, and every guy knew that he was getting some later that night.

Ali and the limo were waiting out front as LeBaron and Phoenix made their way through the crowd of smiling faces. A young lady in a tight black dress and braids that hung past her hem said to her friend, "She better hold on to him, girl."

"Don't you worry," Phoenix said, overhearing her. "He ain't going nowhere."

Ali closed the door after them and said to the woman, "Psst? Ever get jiggy with an Arabian?" She sucked her teeth and flung her braids over her shoulder as she walked off. "She's lucky we're not in Riyadh, I'd have her ass in the trunk," Ali said to himself while he got into the limo, buckled his seat belt and pulled off.

"Sequoia's? I'm impressed," Phoenix said as the limo pulled into the restaurant's circular driveway.

"Dang," LeBaron said. "That's the third time I've impressed you tonight. I'm on a roll."

"You have definitely scored some major cool points tonight."

"Sweetheart, the game ain't over yet; I still got a couple of plays left to run."

Stepping out of the limousine, Phoenix gave him a wicked smile and said, "Play on, playa."

A Saturday night reservation at Sequoia was normally hard to come by. It's the seafood restaurant of choice for D.C.'s weekend club set. LeBaron had had to make reservations three weeks in advance, but anyone who has ever eaten there will testify that it's worth the wait. The restaurant's atmosphere was designed for romance. The tables were spaced widely apart, and the room was dimly lit, perfect for private conversations. The waitstaff discreetly stood just out of view, eyeing everything and nothing at all. Outside, the tables faced the Potomac River, and customers were treated on weekends to a beautiful view of the many yachts anchored nearby.

It was a comfortable seventy-five degrees, so LeBaron and Phoenix requested a table outside.

"I'm starving," LeBaron said. "I already know what I want."

"And what's that, Daddy?" Phoenix seductively drawled.

"Don't start nothing you can't finish at this table." LeBaron winked at Phoenix. "I'm getting the lobster."

"Me too, that's what I want."

"Quit trying to be like me," LeBaron kidded.

Phoenix got a kick whenever he played with her like that. She rolled her neck like she was straight out of the 'hood. "Ain't nobody trying to bite your li'l weak 'bama style."

"' 'Bama? Yo' pappy."

"At least I got one."

"Good one, you got me," he said, laughing. LeBaron usually let her get the last word when they played the dozens; he thought it made her feel good. She knew it but still thought it was so cute. Their little joke session, however, was cut short when their waiter barged into their conversation.

"Good evening, my name is Chahles, and I'll be your waiter this evening." The waiter spoke in a fake British accent, and he overemphasized all of his words, especially his name. It was obvious by his rigid demeanor that he was not in a good mood.

Sensing this, the couple kicked each other under the table and together said, "Hello, Chahles."

He looked at the both of them with an icy diva-with-an-attitude glare. "Do we know what we want to order, or do we need assistance?"

"We would like lobster," LeBaron said, trying his hardest not to laugh in Chahles' face.

"But of course. Will we have anything to drink?"

"Yes," LeBaron continued. "A bottle of white wine."

"May I suggest the Chateau Lafitte, 1969."

"Is that the year or the price?" LeBaron joked. Chahles pursed his lips and gave LeBaron a pitiful look.

After a few seconds Phoenix broke the silence. "Chateau Lafitte will be fine." After Chahles left with their orders, they erupted in muted laughter. "What a tight ass."

"No, baby," LeBaron said, "I don't think so. And he know his momma named him Charles."

Phoenix loved the sweet taste of the lobster, but tonight she didn't really have much of an appetite. She looked across the table at LeBaron, who was eating like he was at the Last Supper. *How could he be so calm?* she thought. The night was winding down, and her stomach was in nervous knots. She had bats instead of butterflies. Bolstering her nerves by downing her second glass of wine, she said, "LeBaron, baby, this has been the best night of my life."

"Me too," he said with a mouthful of food.

"No, I mean really, I'm so in love with you."

Putting down his fork, he looked at her and said, "I love you too, baby." Sensing that the mood was right, he figured now was as good a time as ever for her present. He reached inside his jacket and pulled out a folded piece of paper.

LeBaron cleared his throat, unfolded the paper, and looked deep into Phoenix's eyes. "Phoenix, we've been together for three beautiful years. We've had our ups and downs, but our love carried us through the storms. I've never loved anyone the way I love you. It's God, then you. Without you I am lost. I wrote you a poem that best describes how I feel about you." Phoenix held back the lump forming in her throat as LeBaron began reading.

PHOENIX
I long for the warmth
 and safety of infinite bliss
Never again to know pain,
 An eternal life filled with the memories
 of your tender kiss

Earth and sky may pass
 But a beauty like yours shall remain
To wipe away the tears
 And heal the wounds of life's perpetual pain

There is no fruit as tasty
 no nectar as sweet
As the flavor that is created
 whenever our lips meet

I don't know how long my body
   will be committed to earth
Or what treasures are stored in heaven for me
   because of my work's worth

But out of all the things I've done
   or all the things left for me to do
The greatest joy of my life
   was falling in love with you

"No one has ever said such beautiful things to me," Phoenix said as she dabbed a napkin to her moist eyes.

He smiled and leaned closer. LeBaron then pulled out a box from his breast pocked and held it in his palm. "I have one more beautiful thing for you."

Phoenix's heart beat like an African drum. She had waited three long years for this night. "Close your eyes and give me your hand." She did as told. Phoenix smiled as she heard the hinge on the tiny box squeak.

LeBaron proudly placed the box in her palm. "You can open them now."

She stared, speechless, at the open box. Smiling, he said, "Go ahead, baby, say something."

"Earrings?"

"Uh . . . yeah," LeBaron faltered. "Don't you like them?"

"A fucking pair of earrings?"

"Hey, calm down. What's wrong with you? Those earrings cost me seven thousand dollars."

"I don't give a fuck how much they cost!"

"Lower your voice." Customers at nearby tables turned to look at Phoenix's raucous display, but she didn't care.

"Don't tell me to lower my damn voice! These people don't fucking know me!"

"Phoenix, what in the—"

"I don't believe this shit. I've given the best three years of my life to your tired ass. And for what? A fucking pair of earrings? I deserve more than that."

"Wh-what did you expect?" LeBaron stuttered.

"You know what?" she said, throwing the box at him. "I got just what I should have expected from your trifling ass—nothing. I tell you what, I'm not expecting anything else, and you know something else, mister? You better not either, because I'm through with your ass. I knew I shouldn't have believed Bridgitte."

"Bridgitte? Did she tell you that I bought you an engagement ring?"

She was crying again, but this time they were tears of anger and hurt. "Don't worry about what she told me. Y'all niggas are all the same; you want the coochie but without the commitment. You're no better than your tired-assed boy Eric. You need to see a therapist and get your shit together or you won't be good for any woman. I don't know what I was thinking. God, I told my mother and all of my friends that you were going to propose to me. I'm such a fool."

"No you're not, baby. Please stop crying."

Standing up, she threw her glass of wine in his face. "That's the last time you tell me to do anything. I'm leaving for Paris tomorrow, and when I get back you can come get your shit from my house, then forget my number." She grabbed her purse and stormed off.

"How are you getting home?" LeBaron asked the back of her head.

"Huh? You better ask yourself that question," she shot back at him. She walked out of Sequoia and quickly found the limousine out front. Ali was asleep across the front seat when Phoenix knocked loudly on the window. He scrambled to get up after he saw her through the dark tinted glass.

"Home, Ali," she barked when he jumped out of the limo.

"Yes, Miss Phoenix, is there a prob—"

"Shut up and just drive me home, please." After Ali closed the door, she grabbed her cell phone out of her purse and called Bridgitte.

"Hey, girl," Bridgitte said, looking at the caller ID. "I've been waiting on your call. All I wanna know is how many carats?"

"He gave me a fucking pair of earrings."

"What?"

"You heard me, a lousy set of earrings."

"Oh damn, girl. I'm sorry."

"Don't be. I'm the one who is sorry I ever met his ass."

"Phoenix, you don't mean that."

"The hell I don't, I broke up with him."

"No, you didn't?"

"Yep, and you know what hurt me almost as much as him not proposing, it is that he didn't even remember that he gave me earrings for my birthday."

"That's fucked up. But wait, you're leaving for Paris tomorrow. Don't leave like this. You'll regret it."

"Girl, I don't care."

"You want me to come over?"

"No, I want to be by myself, I have a lot of thinking to do, but you can do me a favor."

"Anything."

"Can you take me to the airport tomorrow? LeBaron was supposed to, but, well—"

"Of course. Don't even worry about that."

"Could you be at my house at eight?"

"OK, I'll be there."

"Thanks, Bridge."

"OK. Bye, girl. It's gonna be all right," Bridgitte consoled Phoenix.

"Girl, please. I'm all right now," Phoenix lied. "See you in the morning."

Bridgitte hung up the phone and started crying. Her heart hurt for her friend, and she felt partly responsible for this mess.

Phoenix snapped her cell phone shut. She felt foolish and betrayed. *How could he give me earrings again?* she thought. *Am I overreacting?* She searched the wetbar for a tissue to wipe her face but the tray was empty. Ali had forgotten to restock it. In frustration she yelled, "Fuck him." She then leaned back in her seat and cried, mascara staining her hot cheeks.

Inside the restaurant, LeBaron sat at the table, dazed, with tears and wine running down his face.

Chapter Ten

"What? She broke up with you? What the fuck for? Was the ring too small?" Eric joked. The last person he'd expected to hear from on this particular Sunday morning was LeBaron.

"I didn't give her the ring. I took it back and exchanged it for earrings." LeBaron's voice cracked.

"You what? Man, get out of here, quit lying. It's too early for jokes."

I'm serious."

"Why the fuck did you take it back?"

"I just couldn't go through with it. I thought about what you said, what my mom said, what everybody said."

"LeBaron, I'm sorry, you're my ace boon; I shouldn't have said anything. I feel responsible."

"Don't be, bruh. I'm a grown-ass man, and maybe this was how it was supposed to be," LeBaron said through a smoke screen of pride.

"Well, you know what I say, what was meant to be will be." Eric attempted to sound sincere.

"Yeah, I guess."

"You try calling her?"

"Yeah, but she didn't pick up the phone."

"Then why ain't you over there?"

"She's gone. Remember she's going to Paris for two weeks."

"Two weeks? Aw that's fucked up. Women; she knew that shit would mess with you too."

"And you know what else? She told me to see a therapist," LeBaron admitted.

"A fucking shrink? Shit, she's the crazy one who turned down an expensive piece of jewelry. By the way, how much them earrings cost?"

"Seven thousand."

"What? Seven G's!" Eric said, eyes bugging. "She needs a damn shrink. Anyway, fuck that, black men don't see therapists."

"Why not?"

"Because we're born crazy and gonna die crazy. It's our heritage to deal with fucked-up situations on our own, and we don't need no fucking Prozac. We got better shit."

"What's that?"

"It's called getting drunk and looking at half-naked bitches. Now that's what you need. You down?"

"Nah, I'ma chill. I'm not in the mood to waste no money on strippers. I got a lot of thinking to do."

"You sure? First lap dance on me."

"I'm good, man. I'll probably take a few days off, though."

"You going on vacation?"

"Nah, I'm just gonna stay here and assess some things."

"All right then. Hey, you hungry? I'll come scoop you and we can go down to Georgia Brown's and get some bougie soul food."

"Nah, I'm not hungry."

"Can't sleep, can't work, can't eat? Nigga, don't go getting all R. Kelly on me. You gon' be watching *Oprah* too?"

"You're trippin', I'm cool."

"Well, holla at me if you want to get out."

"A'ight, peace." LeBaron hung up the phone and walked over to his desk. He sat in his custom-made leather chair and stared at the ceiling.

You need to see a therapist. Phoenix's words had been ringing in his ears ever since she'd uttered them. *Maybe he did*, he thought. He wasn't getting any help from his friends or family. It might help to talk with a professional. LeBaron quickly picked up the phone and started dialing before he could think about what he was doing.

"Hello. Fox 5, Sheila speaking," Sheila, the guest booker for Fox, sang into the receiver.

"Sheila, LeBaron."

"Hey, LeBaron, what do you need on a Sunday?"

"Um . . . uh . . . Remember that doctor we had on last month? He had that wacky married couple on with him?

Um . . . You know, the relationship guy. What's his name, Dr. . . ?

"Carter," Sheila said, refreshing his memory. "Dr. Leighton Carter."

"Yeah, yeah, that's him, how can I get in touch with him?"

"Oh no. Not you, LeBaron."

"Nah . . . nah . . . I um . . . know somebody who . . . uh . . . wants him to speak at a black-tie function."

"Oh . . . OK," Sheila said, the smirk on her face coloring her voice. "I'm looking through my Rolodex. Here it is, it's his office, though."

"That's fine."

LeBaron scribbled the number down quickly, then hung up the phone. He looked at the piece of paper with Dr. Carter's name and number for a few minutes. "I don't need no damn therapist," he said, crumpling up the paper and throwing it in the trash. But trash pickup wasn't until Tuesday.

Chapter Eleven

"Sorry," the receptionist said, "Dr. Carter isn't accepting any new patients." Angela Diaz, Dr. Carter's part-time receptionist and a full-time psychology student at Howard University, had been saying this to callers for the past month.

"You see, I met him recently—" LeBaron pleaded.

"Sir, I'm sor—" she cut him off.

"Miss, this is serious. He'll remember me. Tell him I met him at Fox."

"Hold on a second. I'll see what I can do." Angela put her hand over the phone and turned to Dr. Carter, whispering, "Can you please see this guy? He says he met you at Fox, and he sounds pitiful."

"I know who it is," Dr. Carter whispered. "Tell him to come in tomorrow at noon."

Angela returned the phone to her ear. "Sir, is tomorrow at noon okay?"

"Sure, no problem. I'll be there," LeBaron said.

She wrote his name down in the appointment book, then hung up. Angela had to reach around Dr. Carter to put the phone back in its cradle, but she almost slipped and fell to the floor. It was always a challenge hanging up the phone when she was sitting in his lap.

Dr. Leighton Carter was in need of therapy himself. He was in the midst of a separation from Tina, his wife of ten years: She had caught him having sex in his office with twenty-two-year-old Angela. He had met Angela after he'd lectured at a campus seminar in the spring. He'd been enthralled by her long black hair, mocha brown skin, and exotic features, courtesy of her black and Mexican pedigree. But aside from her beauty, she was an intelligent, driven young woman whom he'd ended up talking to for hours after the lecture had ended. Angela had never cared much for older men, but after hearing the passionate words of Dr. Carter, she'd known she was born to be his. Later that night at dinner she'd asked him about an internship and had walked away with a job that would soon turn into an affair with a married man.

Although he had fast become one of the country's foremost relationship therapists, Dr. Carter was one of those rare people who gave out the world's greatest advice but failed to take heed themselves. In fifteen years of practice, his patient load had become a burden; he'd grown dissatisfied with patients who he believed didn't have any real problems but who felt better knowing they were seeing a therapist. Dr. Carter was getting bored and longed for the good old days when the pains of his patients became his. He used to get so excited when he would diagnose a condition, and he would study and research for days until he could come up with a treatment. But nowadays with the Internet, talk-show therapy, and thousands of self-help books on the market, the world was able to make itself sick one day then cure itself the next. It no longer looked to him for a cure but as a crutch. So in recent months Dr. Carter had begun to cut his caseload. He exclusively accepted patients who challenged him not only professionally but also emotionally. This was how Dr. Carter believed it should be, because the true nectar of life was emotion.

Chapter Twelve

The maxim "Paris is for lovers" was true, Phoenix thought as she sipped cappuccino at an outdoor café near the Eiffel Tower. She marveled at the couples holding hands and kissing as they strolled through the tower's terraced park. Paris may have been for lovers, but its beauty only made Phoenix feel empty.

Phoenix willed herself to keep it together. It was her first full day in Paris, and she was here for business, not to lament over her shambles of a love life. Maxine De La Croix, Phoenix's boss, had insisted that they arrive in Paris a few days before the start of Fashion Week. She wanted everything to be organized ahead of time in order for them to get the maximum amount of schmoozing in. But it was obvious that all the organizing was going to be done by Phoenix. Maxine had been to hundreds of these events around the world; they were like reunions to her. Maxine knew everybody, and everybody knew Maxine. She was a real-life Joan Collins. The fifty-two-year-old mother of three had been married to four different multimillionaires and had had five different plastic surgeries. She certainly got her money's worth, because she looked like a fifty-two-year-old Pamela Anderson.

Maxine was also very powerful as the head buyer for Saks Fifth Avenue of Chevy Chase. It was the second most profitable Saks next to New York. Phoenix was Maxine's protégée. Maxine constantly bragged to her friends and clients about how beautiful, smart, and well-bred Phoenix was. She wanted to groom Phoenix into an African-American version of herself—although there could only be one Maxine De La Croix.

Maxine functioned on her own clock. On the morning of their flight she was late meeting Phoenix at the Lufthansa ticket counter. Phoenix hadn't worried, because no matter where Maxine went, she always arrived fifteen minutes late—just enough time to make an entrance. Yesterday had been no different. Maxine had arrived at the ticket counter with three skycaps carrying nine Louis Vuitton suitcases. The two women had been seated together in the largest first class Phoenix had ever seen. It had been bigger than the first floor of her town house. The triple-decker airbus had even had an elevator that led up to a cigar and brandy lounge. Settling back in the huge leather recliner, Maxine had ordered a Bloody Mary from the flight attendant.

"Maxine, it's ten in the morning," Phoenix had said.

"Oh, really?" Maxine had responded. "That late, huh? In that case, miss, make that a double." It had been classic Maxine. Phoenix had sighed and reclined in her seat, not amused at Maxine's antics. "Dahling, what's wrong you? We're on our way to Paris, you should be smiling."

"I broke up with my boyfriend last night," Phoenix had said, holding back fresh tears threatening to spill from her weary eyes.

"So what's the problem? You should be celebrating."

"Celebrating?" Phoenix blinked, not understanding where Maxine was going with this.

"Of course, you do know what men are good for, don't you?"

"What, Max?"

"Nothing." Maxine had laughed the carefree laugh of a woman who didn't ever have to lie. "Phoenix, we are going to have so much fun and spend so much of the company's money that you won't have time to so much as think of your ex-boyfriend."

But as Phoenix sat there at the café stirring her second cappuccino, she hoped that Maxine was right, but she knew in her heart that two weeks in Paris couldn't make her forget about LeBaron. That is until she saw Maxine walking toward her with the most attractive brother Phoenix had ever seen.

Chapter Thirteen

"Phoenix Morgan, I'd like you to meet Chance," Maxine said.

"Pleasure to meet you, Chance," Phoenix said, shaking his strong, well-manicured hand. Her eyes subtly traveled along his six-foot-four-inch chocolate-covered frame. "Chance, huh? That's a beautiful name."

"Thank you," he replied through a sexy smile. "I guess my name and your face have something in common, because you too are beautiful." He bent slightly to kiss her hand. When his lips touched her hand, Phoenix's insides turned to oatmeal.

"Phoenix, dear?" Maxine said, snapping her out of her Chance trance. "Chance is modeling for Jean-Paul Gaultier next week, and he could use someone to sightsee with while he's in town. I thought you would be the perfect escort." Maxine's eyes glimmered when she saw the way that Chance looked at Phoenix. She mentally patted herself on the back.

"Me? But . . . but I don't know anything about Paris," Phoenix stammered.

"Oh, but I do." Chance's deep baritone dripped with flirtation.

Ooh, Phoenix thought. *His voice is so sexy, and my God those shoulders, those arms, those thighs.*

"It's settled, then," Maxine said. "I'll see you two later, I'm off to a pajama party at Yves St. Laurent's mansion." Turning to walk away, she said, "Don't do anything I wouldn't do." She paused, then continued, "I take that back, because I'll do anything." She winked at Phoenix and left in a flash of crimson silk.

"May I have a seat?" Chance said, diverting his full attention to Phoenix.

"Of course."

Chance sat down and pulled his chair closer to Phoenix. Phoenix averted her eyes to her cappuccino cup. "So, Chance, how do you know Maxine?"

"You're kidding me? Everybody knows Maxine. But, no, she helped get me discovered."

"Really?" Phoenix said.

"Really." He crossed his legs and smiled.

My goodness, Phoenix thought.

"But I don't think you want to know all the arty particulars."

"Try me," Phoenix said before she realized how she

sounded as Chance raised an eyebrow. "I mean . . . please, do tell." Phoenix blushed, cleaning up her comment.

"Maxine discovered me three years ago at a ladies-only birthday party for Tyra Banks in Beverly Hills."

Now it was Phoenix's turn to raise an eyebrow. "Ladies only? So what were you doing there then?" She raised her cup of cappuccino to her lips and took a slow sip.

Chance smiled his perfect smile again. "Well, I was part of the entertainment."

Phoenix almost choked on her cappuccino.

"Are you OK?" Chance asked, concerned.

Phoenix coughed and gathered herself to answer. "I'll be fine. What kind of entertainment, Chance?"

"You're talking to a former member of the Magnificent Seven troop of male dancers. My name was Come Take a Chance."

Phoenix's eyes widened at his revelation. *I'd like to take a Chance*, Phoenix thought.

"Maxine took one look at my six pack and said that I was so cut that I needed to wear a shirt made out of Band-Aids."

Phoenix laughed at the thought of Maxine making such a bold statement. "Yeah, that sounds like Maxine, all right."

"At first I wondered what this white woman wanted with me. I could usually tell from their eyes that they wanted more than a dance, but Maxine was different. After our show she gave me her card and said, 'Dahling, you are too classy to shake your ass for money. With that bone structure and physique, you can make more money than you can fathom and keep your clothes on. Well, most of them, at least.' "

"Yeah, that sounds like Maxine once again." Phoenix smiled, shaking her head.

"I know, right. So I marinated on what she said for a couple of days and gave her a call, and the rest is, well, history, or in the case of Maxine, *herstory*."

"Wow, that's impressive."

"Maxine is impressive. If it weren't for her, I wouldn't be where I am now." Chance leaned in and lightly touched Phoenix's hand. "Sitting here with you."

Phoenix drew her hand back and patted at her perfectly styled hair. "Woo! This breeze is something, isn't it?"

Noting her cue, Chance leaned back in his chair and changed the conversation.

"How'd you get a beautiful name like Phoenix?"

"Well, my mother had complications the entire time that she was pregnant with me. She almost lost me three times, but somehow I kept hanging in there. According to her, each time I rose like a phoenix."

"That's beautiful."

"And what about you? Chance is a rather unique name."

"My parents are rather unique individuals. They already had six grown children, and the day after my pop's fiftieth birthday my mom told him that she wanted to have another baby."

"How old was she?"

"Forty-nine."

Phoenix's mouth dropped open. "Whoa."

"Tell me about it. So they prayed for one more chance to have a child, and the following year I was born."

"Aw, that's so special."

"Yeah, Moms and Pops just celebrated their fifty-fifth anniversary last month. They still act like newlyweds. Oh . . . I'm sorry."

"Why are you sorry?" Phoenix looked confused.

"Don't be upset, but Maxine told me about your situation."

"She what?" Phoenix said a little louder than she wanted to.

"Now calm down. She only told me because she's worried about you and she wants you to make the most out of this trip. It's important for your career that you have fun here and mingle, make contacts, and not be chained down with heartache."

"Oh, and I guess that's where you come in, huh, Mr. Chance?"

"That's right, I'll help you rise once again, Ms. Phoenix."

Damn, he's good, Phoenix thought, noticing the sincerity in his eyes. *Damn good.*

Chapter Fourteen

"This is a terrible idea," LeBaron said to himself as he sat in his parked car in front of the modest brick town house. "Eric was right, I should just say fuck this." The conversation with Eric was still strong in his mind. He still couldn't believe that he was actually about to see a therapist. But the thought of losing Phoenix forever gave him the motivation to get out of his car and walk through the doors of Dr. Carter's office.

"Hello, sir, you must be Mr. Brown. My name is Angela, how are you today?"

Forcing a smile, he said, "I'm hoping Dr. Carter can tell me."

After signing in with Angela, LeBaron sat down and thumbed nervously through an old issue of *Sports Illustrated*.

Angela just smiled at him; she had seen that nervous look on many patients.

After about ten minutes, Angela got up and walked into Dr. Carter's office. She soon after opened the door and said, "Mr. Brown, you can come in now and have a seat. Dr. Carter will be with you in a moment."

"Thanks," LeBaron muttered as he entered the empty office.

Watching from behind a two-way mirror, Dr. Carter observed LeBaron. He routinely watched his new patients for a few minutes before meeting with them. Years of experience had taught him that he could learn a lot about a person by the way they behaved when alone.

LeBaron fidgeted, his eyes darting around the spacious and elegantly decorated office. Restless with anxiety, he got up and walked around. The sofa and chairs were deep mahogany brown, and the desk was a heavy oak. Original paintings by Ernie Barnes—and even an original Andy Warhol—hung on the walls. There were framed photographs of Dr. Carter with everyone from Oprah Winfrey to President Clinton. Isolated on the wall above Dr. Carter's desk hung three degrees from Georgetown University.

As LeBaron looked around, he thought it strange that Dr. Carter didn't have any books. If he had asked Angela, she would have told him that Dr. Carter didn't read books, he read people.

LeBaron was so intrigued by a crystal ball on Dr. Carter's desk that he didn't notice him walk into the room.

"You know, LeBaron, love is like a crystal ball, the closer you get to it, the cloudier it gets," Dr. Carter said as he looked out of his window.

LeBaron jumped. "Damn, you scared me."

"I scare myself sometimes," Dr. Carter said as he released a hearty laugh. He shook LeBaron's hand and sat down at his desk. "Please, have a seat."

LeBaron was taken aback by Dr. Carter's green eyes. He hadn't noticed them before and thought it strange that someone as brown as he was could have eyes that color. "They're real," Dr. Carter said. "But you didn't come here to find out about me, you came here to find out why you're here."

"Well, if you remember . . . Phoenix, that's my girl-friend. She left me, and it's driving me crazy."

"Why did she leave you?"

"Because I didn't ask her to marry me."

"You didn't or couldn't?"

LeBaron rubbed his chin. "I guess you can say I couldn't."

"Why not?"

"Honestly, Doc, I have no idea." Dr. Carter didn't speak: he let the silence act as a motivator. LeBaron continued, "See, deep down I know I want to marry her, but I'm scared."

"Scared of what?"

"I think I'm scared of spending the rest of my life with the same woman."

"Do you love Phoenix?"

"Of course I do."

"Why do you love her?"

"Well, she's cool, you know? Everything that a man can ask for. She's smart and independent, understanding and supporting."

"Does she cook?" Dr. Carter said, smiling.

LeBaron laughed. "Like a grandmother."

"Well, then," Dr. Carter said, "if you don't want her, I'll take her." They shared more laughter, but then he got serious. "Does she listen to your problems and stresses?"

"Yes," LeBaron said.

"Do you sleep better when she's with you?"

"Like a baby."

"Since she left you, how have you felt?"

"Hell, Doc, look at me. How do you think I feel? It's been three days and I feel like shit. I need a shave, and I can't eat or sleep."

"Now, LeBaron, pardon me for being frank, but what you just told me sounds like bullshit. Phoenix seems like the kind of woman any man would want. Now either she is real fucked up or you are. If I am going to help, you have to be honest with me and tell me the real reason why you can't marry her."

LeBaron sunk into the chair and pondered Dr. Carter's words. After a lengthy pause, he said, "I don't trust women."

"Here we go." Dr. Carter threw his hands up in the air.

"Quit blaming it on women. LeBaron, you don't trust yourself."

"That's bullshit," LeBaron said. "I know who I am."

"Have you ever cheated on her?"

"What do you mean by cheating?"

"Have you ever slept with another woman?" Dr. Carter said.

"No, but I think about it sometimes."

"Why?"

LeBaron shrugged his shoulders. "I've always been like that, I mean all men have those thoughts, right?"

Ignoring him, Dr. Carter continued probing. "Do you know what love is?"

"Yeah, I think so."

"Is Phoenix the first woman that you've ever been in love with?"

A devilish smirk crept onto LeBaron's lips. "No."

"How many then?"

"I don't know, a few."

"Well, LeBaron, the first thing I need you to do is tell me about all the women you've loved."

"All the women I've loved, huh?"

"That's right. Why don't we move over to the couch?"

I was in the seventh grade the first time I fell in love. I was walking to my locker when I saw Dionne Gilliam. She caught my eye because she was the first girl I had ever seen wearing those new jellies sandals. They were made out of bright red plastic, and they matched the polish on her pretty toes. It looked like she dipped her big toe in strawberry jam, my favorite flavor next to grape Kool-Aid. She was also wearing the hell out of a pair of white Chic no-pocket jeans. Very few twelve-year-old girls could pull that off with her finesse. Rounding off her ensemble was a T-shirt so tight that it had to belong to her baby sister. I was almost scared to look at her face because I knew that if she was ugly I was going to commit suicide on the spot. But, luckily for the janitor and me, God doesn't make mistakes.

She walked by me and our eyes met for the shortest second ever recorded. We smiled and said hi to each other. Not only did this girl have a great future in front of her, if you know what I mean, but her hips took my young mind on long trips. I couldn't get her out of my mind as I walked in a daze to my health class and took my usual seat in the back. Just as Mrs. Jessup was about to begin the day's lecture on hygiene for armpits, the door opened, and it was her.

"Class, I'd like you to meet a new student, say hello to Dionne," Mrs. Jessup said. "Hello, Dionne," came back a chorus of twelve-year-olds. It was my lucky day. I was looking sharp, too. I had on my brand-new blue-and-white Chuck Taylor All Star sneakers, a pair of tight-ass Jordache jeans, and a fake light blue Polo shirt. My shirt was so fake that it looked like the Polo guy was riding a giraffe. My hair was brushed back and greased with about a half a can of Murray's pomade. I had so many waves in my hair people would get seasick looking at them. Dionne walked past me, and a glint of recognition crossed her face. She mouthed "Hi," but I didn't respond. I was too busy thinking of how pretty our children would be.

I planned on talking to her after class, but the line was too long. So I decided to play the background for the next two weeks. Whenever she walked by I'd look the other way. Shit, I almost got a hernia from trying to hold my neck muscles still. But my plan was working, because she started going out of her way by week three to talk to me.

I had to think this one out. Play it cool, you know, because I had a habit of fucking things up. But not this time. I knew the guys had thrown every line in the book at her, so I had to be creative. I found my angle with relative ease. I was always a fan of music, especially the classic R&B ballads, you know, "old folks' music." Sunday mornings in the Brown household were like oldies night at the club. All morning long I'd be messing up the words to songs by the Isley Brothers, Teddy Pendergrass, and Peabo Bryson. But my main man was Barry White. I always wanted to talk to women the way he did. But at the age of twelve I didn't have many opportunities to tell a girl "Take off that brassiere, my dear"; it would been more like "Take off that training bra, li'l ma." Then again I could've said that to Dionne, because yes indeedy she had enough to feed the greedy.

After watching other boys in the school get dissed in the

few weeks that Dionne had been there, I decided it was now time for me to make my move. One day in science class I slipped her a note. It wasn't that old, tired-ass "If you like me check yes or no in the box." It was some highly evolved Don Juan type of shit. I filled the note with some poetry and even sprayed some of my Dad's Old Spice on the sheet of notebook paper. She didn't seem to mind the round cologne stain on the paper either. She seemed excited that I was even talking to her. I played it off even though my insides were having a nuclear meltdown. I could tell she liked the note by the way her eyes widened and she said, "You really mean that?" I managed to squeak out, "With all my heart."

From that moment Dionne was hooked, and I was cooked. About once a week I would give her a special note. She'd read each one with a smile. Her smiles evolved into hugs and her hugs into kisses on the cheek. I'd carry her books while walking her to class and home from school. I'd even walk by her other classes and wave to her through the small window on the door until the teacher would give me that get-the-hell-away-from-my-door look. I started ditching my boys so Dionne and I could eat lunch together, and I even shared those good-ass cafeteria biscuits with her. At night we'd talk on the phone for hours, or until my dad would get on the phone and bark, "LeBaron, it's nine o'clock, you know what that means?" I'd be thinking, *Yeah, I know what it means. Once again it's "let's cock block LeBaron time."*

It was my poetry-filled, Old-Spice-scented notes that won her affections. She told me she'd never had a guy say those things before. She said it reminded her of those guys on the radio singing to their women. I smiled and didn't divulge my secret. After all, what she didn't know wouldn't hurt me.

Well about a month passed since the beginning of my letter-writing campaign. I was in homeroom feeling like the man. I'd mowed a few more yards and was able to upgrade my footwear to some fresh red-and-white pleather Converse Dr. J's. I was the only one in the seventh grade with them, so I knew I had it going on. And with Dionne as my woman, what more could a young playa ask for?

So there I sat in the back of homeroom holding court, lying about my sexual experience with women. Hell, the closest I had ever come to seeing a naked woman was when I walked into the bathroom and caught my mother drying herself off. That's when Dionne walked in and made a bee-line straight toward me. Normally I would have welcomed watching her walk in any direction, but she had an angry look in her eyes. This day she wore pink jellies with matching toenail polish. She also had on a tight pink miniskirt with a pink-and-white paisley blouse. But the icing on that pink-and-white slice of girl-cake was her freshly done, long, silky California Curl. She must have spritzed half a bottle of activator to get it to glisten that morning. I briefly wondered if somebody told her what I said we did behind my garage. It was a small schoolboy lie that I didn't have to tell; besides, we didn't even have a garage.

"LeBaron, what the hell is this?" She held out a familiar-looking and -smelling piece of paper. The entire class stopped what they were doing and looked at us. You could hear a feather drop in the room.

Looking around the class of interested eyes and ears, I managed to answer, "Uh . . . One of the poems I gave you." I immediately regretted letting that tidbit slip, because my boys screamed "Poems?" in a harmony so tight Boyz II Men would have been jealous.

Dionne said, "Negro, this ain't yours." Mass laughter from my classmates followed.

"Uh . . . yes, it is," I replied rather weakly. You could hear my pride drop now; even the teacher was interested in the preteen drama unfolding in her homeroom.

"Stop lying! My momma read this, and you know what she told me?"

No, I thought, but if I had to guess, it wasn't, "Dionne, go to class tomorrow and clown this young boy."

Trampling over my thoughts, she said, "My momma said that these are lines from a Barry White song."

"No, they ain't," I defended myself and technically that was true—it was from the Isley Brothers. The class was cracking up. I felt like I was in a fun house with all the mirrors and the weirdly distorted heads of my classmates were laughing at me.

"Don't call me anymore," she said while she stuffed the letter in my face and stomped off.

By the third period the whole school had heard about it.

I was thoroughly humiliated. Heartbroken, I walked home from school by myself.

Later that evening my dad noticed my long face, and I told him about the fiasco that was my day. "Son, you learned a valuable lesson today. Would you like to tell me what it was?" My dad killed me, because he'd always ask me these kinds of questions.

"Next time I should find an older band to steal my lyrics from?"

Affectionately, he replied, "No, dummy, the lesson is that you have to be original. Next time say it from the heart, not from the radio." My dad's wisdom stuck with me, because after that I started writing my own poetry.

"It's funny, a few years ago I ran into Dionne at our ten-year high school reunion, and guess what?"

"What?" Dr. Carter asked. He rested his Montblanc on the legal pad he had been busily jotting down notes on.

"She asked me to call her."

"Why am I not surprised?" Dr. Carter chuckled. "Can you compare what you felt with Dionne to the feelings you have for Phoenix?"

"There's no comparison," LeBaron said matter-of-factly.

"But I asked you to tell me about the women you've loved."

"Well I guess I didn't really love Dionne. I was infatuated. It was puppy love."

"Well, thank you for sharing your first experience with

puppy love. I'd like you to tell me about your first sexual experience."

"Alone or with someone else?" LeBaron quipped.

Dr. Carter just shook his head, picked his pen back up, and turned to a fresh page.

I was fifteen when I lost my virginity. It was 1984, the year George Orwell predicted would be mankind's last. Well, the world didn't end, but my innocence did. Her name was Charmagne, but it should have been Champagne, because the first time I saw her she made me feel all bubbly inside. Charmagne lived around the block from me, and it was as if she was fine china or something, because she'd only be out on special occasions. But this sista was fine. She looked like a young Lola Falana. Her skin was smooth and dark like Hershey chocolate, and her body was shaped like one of those old-fashioned Coke bottles. She had the kind of voice that sounded nice saying anything, even if she was cursing you out. I especially loved the way she used to say, "Kiss my ass, LeBaron," which was something I often day-dreamed about. It was a chance encounter at a junior varsity basketball game that changed my life forever.

Where I'm from, high school sports are like the black Academy Awards, and you must dress to impress. Folks from the Dirty South are famous for their everyday flam-boyance, myself included. So there I was, wearing gray-and-black checkered pants and a white, winged-tip tuxedo shirt. But instead of a bow tie, I wore a gray-and-white leather tie. The foundation for this outfit was a pair of highly buffed gray Stacy Adams dress shoes. I was, as my grandfather used to say, cleaner than the board of health. And when I walked into the gym, all eyes were on me.

Charmagne was with her friends, and when she saw me she looked surprised. She was used to seeing me look grungy in the neighborhood because we were always playing brutal football and basketball games. We ran into each other during halftime, and the first words out of her mouth were, "Damn, LeBaron, you looking kinda fine." With the way that she looked me up and down I felt like I was auditioning for a starring role in a movie—her movie. We exchanged numbers, and I was so happy that I almost did the running man. I couldn't wait to dial those digits. I called her less than an hour after the game. Soon we were talking for hours every night, and then I'd think about her all day. I was so in love with Charmagne. She was very mature for her age—she was fifteen but acted like she was twenty and kissed like she was thirty. We'd kiss for hours at a time. Her lips were the New World, and I was Christopher Columbus. I loved to kiss her neck because she smelled so sweet. Whenever we were alone I had to touch some part of her body, and she wanted me to. After a few weeks of going out we did everything except have sex.

I was really scared to have sex with her. No matter how macho I appeared, I was still a nervous fifteen-year-old virgin. I mean, I barely knew how to pee without getting any on my shoes. I had come close to having sex a few times before, but somehow I'd always managed to mess it up.

Not with Charmagne though: I knew she was my sexual destiny, I just hoped I wouldn't blow it this time.

It happened on a warm summer's afternoon, one of those days when you just knew something good was going to happen. Up until then my best days had revolved around scoring the most points in a pickup basketball game. But this was to be one of those really extra big days. It began when Charmagne called me and said her parents weren't going to be home for hours. I rode my bike over there like I was going for an Olympic gold medal. I was so pressed, I damn near ran into the side of a Taco Bell.

Finally, I got there without injuring myself. I rang the doorbell and Charmagne answered wearing tight blue shorts and a tank top. Her ample breasts reminded me of two smooth coconuts and looked just as sweet. She began kissing me as soon I stepped into the living room, and she wasted no time leading me to her bedroom. When she took off her clothes I wanted to take off running. My heart was beating harder than the LAPD.

After she unzipped my pants and realized how happy I was to see her, I gently, if somewhat clumsily, laid her down on the bed and began kissing her. But she was through with kissing and wanted me to make love to her. I was so nervous I couldn't for the life of me figure out how to do it properly. She said she wanted me to run my fingers all over her body, but I was all thumbs. "No, LeBaron, that's not it," she said on more than one occasion. "Oops," was all that I could say. Frustrated, she finally said, "Let me do it."

She took my ding-a-ling in her hands and guided me inside. "Now thrust," Charmagne commanded. For the next ten minutes I died and went to Charmagne Heaven. She felt so good I wanted to crawl up inside of her and go to sleep. Then I felt this sudden weird sensation in my pelvic area. I had butterflies, and my dick felt like a tube of toothpaste that was squeezed too tight. Then it happened—I came. I thought something was wrong, because I lost control of my senses. A jolt of pure electricity flowed through my body and came through my pores. Then in a flash it went away.

I lay there in a sweaty haze trying to gather my thoughts, and I realized that Charmagne was on top of me, looking into my eyes. And I had one goofy-ass look on my face, too. I didn't know what to say to her. I mean, I didn't even know what was happening, but she did, and she told me that she enjoyed it. It still didn't register with me, all I knew was that I had to leave. My legs were so wobbly I couldn't even ride my bike. I walked it all the way home.

When I walked through the door to my house, I went straight to the bathroom. I looked at my reflection in the mirror. I looked the same, but I wasn't. I felt like a man now. I felt ten feet tall. I knew the secret handshake. I had Just Got Laid written all over my face. And then I threw up. For the rest of the day I kept to myself, trying to make sense of it all.

"Charmagne and I sexed each other for the rest of that summer, and we broke up five months later. It was the typical teenage relationship, with highs and lows. Oddly enough, we've remained friends to this day."

The corners of Dr. Carter's lips curled into a smile. "I'm impressed, you have a vivid memory. I think your encounter with Charmagne was definitely a turning point in your love life."

"How so?"

"LeBaron, perhaps the greatest thing about sex is that first experience. It's a natural high that you experience only once. Maybe that's why we humans are so addicted to sex, always chasing that first high."

"That's right," LeBaron said, "I definitely overdosed on Charmagne."

"You are a very funny storyteller, " Dr. Carter managed to say while laughing.

"I do all right, I guess. But funny stuff always seems to happen to me, especially where women are concerned. What I want to know is why?"

"LeBaron, many people believe that the events in our lives occur by happenstance. Call it chance or any other Western-world-new-age-psycho-mumbo-jumbo term you want to choose. But they're wrong, things don't just happen."

"I don't understand."

"Well, LeBaron, physicists say that for every action there is an equal and opposite reaction. The entire world, whether natural, physical, or chemical, is governed by mathematics, and what happens to us is the product of our actions and reactions. Actions can multiply, add, subtract, and even divide events in our lives."

"Okay, but what does that have to do with what I just told you?"

"For one thing, the confusion and apprehension you are experiencing in your current relationship is directly related to how you handled—or should I say, miscalculated—the situations you just told me about."

LeBaron knitted his eyebrows.

"LeBaron, listen very close to what I am about to ask you. What did you feel when you first saw Dionne in those red jellies? Or Charmagne's Coke bottle body?"

Smiling, LeBaron said, "I guess I felt a funny feeling— all tingly inside; you know, like butterflies?"

"LeBaron, what you felt is the most powerful force on the planet. What you felt is a force that has built empires while at the same time causing them to crumble. You felt an energy that has altered the course of human history. What you felt is the power of a woman.

"A woman is the center of the universe, and her power is directly tied to the forces of the universe."

"So, Leighton, lemme see, what you are saying is—"

"Stop!" Dr. Carter said, interrupting him. "Don't talk. I want you to listen. This power comes from inside a woman's womb and is the very essence of life.

"Women are so very important, more important than even they know. A woman gives life and through her womb travels the light of the Almighty. God chose women to be the bearer of children because a woman is strong, much stronger than a man." LeBaron raised an eyebrow at Dr. Carter's statement.

"Impossible your eyes say, but there are many different kinds of strength. Where we are strong physically, women are strong mentally and spiritually. You can't fight her spiritual power nor misinterpret it as mere sex appeal. You must love your woman for who she really is."

LeBaron lay still on the leather couch. There were no words to speak, no jokes to crack.

"Think about what I told you until I see you again. I'd like you to come in on Friday. We'll talk about men, OK?" Dr. Carter said as he capped his pen, gathered his notes, and left his office.

After a few minutes, LeBaron got up off the couch and walked out. He stopped to confirm his next appointment with Angela.

"I have you down," she said. "Friday at noon."

"He's deep," LeBaron said, turning to walk away. Angela just smiled; it wasn't the first time she'd heard that.

Chapter Fifteen

It had been three days since Eric had last spoken with LeBaron, and he was worried. Instead of a few days, LeBaron had decided to take the entire week off sick. Given the fact that he hadn't missed a day of work in the last four years, it was so unlike him. A few people at the station were concerned and asked Eric if it was anything serious. He deflected the questions by saying that LeBaron was OK and just sick with a stomach virus. But Eric knew that it wasn't an upset stomach but a broken heart that had sidelined his main man. After leaving three messages on LeBaron's machine, Eric decided to stop by after work and drag his friend's depressed ass out of the house.

As Eric pulled into LeBaron's driveway, he wondered if he was out of town. The usually manicured lawn needed a visit from a lawn mower, three editions of the *Washington Post* were on the welcome mat, flyers from local Chinese restaurants were left inside the screen door, and mail over-flowed from the mailbox. "Damn, he must be fucked up," Eric said to himself and sighed as he took it all in and pressed the doorbell. He waited a minute, then banged on the door. "Open up, nigga, it's da Prince George's County police. We got your black ass surrounded," he yelled. After another minute the front door cracked open, revealing half of LeBaron's face.

"Damn, bruh, you look like Frankenstein." Eric leaned in and took a sniff. "And you smell like Dr. Funkenstein."

"Shit," LeBaron laughed, clearing his throat, "I feel like his ass too."

Attempting to push his way through the door, Eric said, "You gon' let me in or what? You're acting like I'm a Jehovah's Witness."

"Sorry, come in, man. I was just chillin'."

"Chillin' my ass. You look like you were just dying." Eric stepped inside and scanned the living room. He was shocked at how junky the house was, as LeBaron was usually such a neat freak. His expensive Italian leather couch was covered with laundry. Dirty socks and underwear were scattered on the floor. Two empty Papa John's pizza boxes, along with an empty liter bottle of Pepsi, littered the coffee table. "Dog, I'm worried about you."

"Worried? I'm all right."

"Man, look at your crib. Shit looks like *Good Times*. Leave it to a nigga to turn a penthouse into the projects."

"I was just about to clean this place up," LeBaron lied.

"Do that shit tomorrow, we're going out for a drink."

"Nah, I don't feel—"

"I don't want to hear that shit. So go lay out your playa clothes, get shaved, and, judging by the way you smell, definitely get yo' nasty ass in the shower."

"A'ight, but call your mama and tell her I'll keep the tub full of bubbles until she gets here."

They arrived at Jefferson's at six o'clock, just before the restaurant's rush hour. Located in the center of George-town, the restaurant was very popular with the after-work crowd. LeBaron and Eric got the last two stools at the bar. Eric took the liberty of ordering them two Cognac and Cokes plus two Pablo Espinoza cigars, freshly imported from the Dominican Republic.

"You know I don't smoke," LeBaron said.

"I know, but this is a special occasion. Besides you don't smoke Espinozas, you puff them."

"What's so special about this occasion?"

"Tonight I'm raising yo' Lazarus ass from the dead."

"Go 'head with that, E."

"Yeah, whatever. So what you been doing with yourself? Everybody's been sweating me about you."

"Really?"

"Yeah," Eric said, cracking a smile. "They think you got AIDS."

LeBaron cut his eyes at Eric. "That shit ain't funny."

"But that look on your face is."

"I went to see a therapist."

"What? You lying?" Eric frowned.

"Square biz, dog. I went to see that guy we had on the morning show last month."

"Who?"

"His name is Dr. Leighton Carter."

"He black?"

"Yeah."

Eric shook his head. "Where did he get his degree from. Devry?"

"There you go. He went to Georgetown."

"How much does he charge?"

"A hundred and fifty dollars an hour."

"Goddamn, what he charge per minute?"

"Eric, if you would have heard what he said you'd agree he's worth it."

"Man, the only person worth one fifty an hour is a highly skilled prostitute."

Laughing, LeBaron said, "You are stupid. Quit playing for a second. He broke down the importance of a woman. He talked about how she's divine and how strong she is."

"Really? I believe that."

"You? Get the fuck outta here."

"Nah, seriously," Eric said, lighting up his cigar. "My last girlfriend Erica was real strong."

"Oh yeah, what made her so strong?"

"She lifted weights."

"See, that's your problem, Eddie Murphy. You don't understand women. To you they're just notches on the bedpost."

"Nah, bruh, I dig what you're saying, but the women you're talking about are few and far between. These honeys out here in D.C. are bed-hopping, man-sharing, baby-daddy-having, trifling gold diggers, and I ain't trying to pay to play. I'll get serious when I find a real woman."

"That's bullshit, you're too busy trying to be the Mack of the Year to notice a good woman even if you tripped over her."

"Boy I tell you," Eric smirked. "A nigga see a shrink one time and all of a sudden he's Sigmund fuckin' Freud. You forget, oh enlightened one, we used to ho together."

"Yeah, I know, but I wasn't happy."

"Well, you ain't got no ho now, and you still ain't happy, so what's the difference?"

"You don't understand."

"I do too." Eric stood up and made a sweeping motion with his right arm. "Look, how can I respect these broads when they all up in my face, titties and ass all hanging out trying to get in my Benz. How can you call a woman like that divine?"

"But see, that's where we come in, man. They only act like that because that's what we want. If we didn't follow our animal instincts and chase 'em like wild game, they wouldn't do it."

Eric sighed loudly. "Ever since you turned in your playa

card you've gotten naïve. Hos have been around since the beginning of time, and as long as they're around I'ma be around 'em. C'mon LB, look at how Phoenix got you acting all sad and shit. You bought her those expensive-ass diamond earrings, which should have been enough to keep you in pussy and pancakes for a year, but no, you also took her to see a sold-out Maxwell show, and you drove her ass around in a limo, and what did you get? Tell me, what did you wind up with? Your dick in your hand at the end of the night, that's what. I tried that shit before, but I ain't going out like that no more. They can go get Babyface for that bullshit."

"See," LeBaron said, "that's what Dr. Carter said. Men get hurt, and then we take it out on every other woman. I'm telling you, dog, you should go to see him."

"What? Now I know you're crazy," Eric said, eyes bugging.

"Seriously, you have some issues to resolve."

"You're the one with the issues. You're over here crying on your pillow, making dedications on the Quiet Storm while Phoenix is in Paris. She's probably laying up in a hotel room fucking Tyson Beckford."

"Eric, there's no hope for you."

Eric stared at his drink. "Whatever, man, let's change the subject; you're making me depressed."

"OK, lover boy, what's up with you?"

"Yo, you won't believe what happened to me Sunday night."

"I probably would."

"Check this, you remember that honey Lauren I've been kicking it with? The dancer?"

"You mean the stripper, don't you?" LeBaron grinned.

"Yeah," Eric said, chuckling. "But she thinks her ass is Debbie Allen. Anyway, she busted me."

"You? Not the playa from the Himalaaaaaayas?"

"Dude, I was slipping, slipping hard."

"What happened?"

"Well, she came to pick me up to go to this play. Uh . . . what was it? Oh yeah, *Mama, I Want a Man* or *Oh Lord, Send Me a Man* or some bullshit like that. So she drives up, and I came out the house to get in her car, but she says she needs to use the bathroom."

"Uh-oh, you had another girl inside?"

"Nah, I ain't that stupid. So anyway, I thought she was going to use the one downstairs, so I waited in the car. But no, her ass had to try and surprise me by going upstairs to leave a present on my dresser."

"Oh shit, what did she find up there?"

"Nothing in the room, but she decided to use the master bathroom, and while she's sitting on the toilet, what do you think she saw in the trash can?"

"A condom?"

"Nope, I could have handled that easily."

"What? What?" LeBaron was getting antsy.

"She found a mother-fuckin' tampon wrapper."

"Damn."

"Yeah, that's what I thought when she got in the car and threw it at me."

"Aw, that's fucked up. What did you tell her?"

"I said that it must have been hers."

"What'd she say?"

"She said that it wasn't her brand which definitely confused a brother. I thought that shit was all the same."

"Nah, potna, females are real particular about that shit."

"Man, I didn't even know that shit was in there."

"So what did she do?"

"She cursed my ass out real nice like."

"Damn, bruh, so she left you, huh?"

"That's the wild shit, son. She fucked me later that night on some old Janet Jacme, porno type shit."

"Get the fuck outta here!"

"Yeah, so there, nigga. I don't need your fancy, expensive-ass doctor, 'cause my shit's legit."

LeBaron finally lit up his cigar and took a deep pull. "Ahh," he exhaled, then coughed. "Nah, your shit's fucked up."

Chapter Sixteen

The morning of LeBaron's next session started badly. He woke up nearly three hours early, his night interrupted by dreams of Phoenix dancing with another man. He couldn't remember the man's face but certainly remembered how it mocked him. As he dressed, the house had an eerie silence. The television was off, and so was the radio. LeBaron always ate breakfast, but he left the house without eating. Walking past the mirror on the way out the door, he also realized that he had forgotten to comb his hair. "What the hell is wrong with me?" he sighed, grabbing a baseball cap, then walking out the door.

LeBaron had forgotten how efficient the Metro was. He took it to avoid traffic but ended up arriving nearly an hour and a half early for his second session with Dr. Carter. He decided to take a short walk, since he had some time to himself. Dr. Carter's office was located on Connecticut Avenue, a few blocks from the National Zoo. After buying a can of Coke from a corner vendor, he headed toward the zoo.

While crossing the street, he heard someone call his name. Turning around, he didn't see anyone familiar, so he kept on walking. Again he heard his name, and this time he turned to see Dr. Carter and Angela walking up the street. They were carrying what looked like carryout bags of Chinese food.

"Hey, Dr. Carter, Angela," LeBaron said once they got closer.

"Hello, LeBaron," Dr. Carter said. "You're a little early."

"I know. I'm always early. I got that from the army. But since I had some time to kill, I thought I would go to the zoo."

"Excellent idea. Mind if I join you?"

"No, but our app—"

"Don't worry about it. Angela can take care of the office, and it'll do me some good to get some fresh air. Besides, there is an animal exhibit I'd like you to see."

"The new pandas?"

"No," Dr. Carter said, "the lions."

For the ten minutes or so it took them to walk to the lions' den, Dr. Carter and LeBaron talked about current events.

As they approached the den, Dr. Carter led LeBaron to a nearby picnic table that provided a great view of the pride. The lions had recently been fed and were now sprawled in the shade.

"What a life," LeBaron said. "Eating, sleeping, and mating."

"Quite a life indeed," Dr. Carter replied. "It's a life a great majority of men spend their lives emulating."

"Hmmm, I never thought of it like that."

Dr. Carter didn't take his eyes off the pride. "You see that male over there, the one with the full mane? He exists for two very simple reasons, to protect and to procreate. If he fails in his first duty he cannot fulfill the latter, thus he loses his lioness, is expelled from his territory and eventually wanders aimlessly until he dies, alone."

LeBaron just nodded; he was beginning to get a feel for when to speak and when not to.

"That's all the lion wants to do. Eat, sleep, and protect his mate. It's instinctual, and man has the same instinct. The human kingdom is a reflection of the animal kingdom. It is only when man allows the superior logic of his advanced brain to override his primeval instinct that he rises above such a routine existence. But sadly many men do not rise above it and spend their lives like a lion, simply eating, sleeping and fucking."

"But why?" LeBaron frowned.

"LeBaron, if I knew the reason I would be God, but since I'm not, I'm left with only a theory."

"What is it?" LeBaron asked.

"I won't tell you until you tell me something first."

"Okay."

"Have you ever thought you were in love, but it really turned out to be lust?"

"Oh yeah, definitely, quite a few times."

"No, I mean really in lust—the kind of lust that nearly drives a man crazy?"

"Quite a few times."

"Tell me about one."

As a teenager, I was always attracted to older women. Older but not wrinkled. Samantha was twenty-seven and anything but wrinkly. Her skin and body were tighter than White House security. She was a five-foot-ten, one hundred-forty-five-pound, coffee-colored Amazon. She always wore her long hair in a ponytail. I called her the ghetto Cindy Crawford because she had a cute little fake mole that she would always draw on. I knew it was a fake because she could never draw it in the same spot twice. Some days it would be so crooked her face would look like a constellation.

We worked the same shift at the Piccadilly Cafeteria on Broad Street in Lake Charles. Samantha prepared food, and I washed pots. While not the most glamorous of occupations, it paid enough to keep my sixteen-year-old ass freshly dipped in the latest fashions from Mitches, New Look Fashion, a popular clothing store where you could get an entire outfit—suit, shirt, ties, belt, socks, shoes and drawers—for sixty-three dollars.

In 1983 my brother Dante was in a commercial for the store, and Mitch is still running the same commercial.

Mitch was a slick Arab who owned the store. Have you ever heard of an Arab named Mitch?

Anyway, the little change I got from my Piccadilly also offset the cost of my real job, which was professional weed smoking. Oh yes, I was a world-class herbalist. I was high most of the time I washed pots. I think that's what made me so good at it. In the words of my friend and colleague, the fry cook D'Wayne, "I was a pot-washing mother-fucker."

Every time Samantha went to the storeroom, I faked like I had to go too, just to be around her. One day I followed her into the pastry freezer. While she reached up to grab a lemon custard pie, I reached out and grabbed her ass. And she didn't say anything! Not a damn word! Even as I held on to one of her ass cheeks for dear life. After about five seconds of silence I felt foolish. A woman sure can make a man feel stupid without saying a word.

"You finished?" she finally said. "Did you get a good feel?"

"Uh . . . yes," I said with a shit-eating grin. "Your ass is soft as toilet paper, and right now I feel like shit."

She laughed that laugh again, but then her voice got real soft as she said, "LeBaron, there is a place and a time for everything, and the place and time to grab my ass is at my house and not when I'm on the clock."

"What's your address and what time do you get off?" I shot back.

"Negro, how old are you?"

"Sixteen and far from green," I said as smoothly as I could.

"We'll see," she said and walked out of the freezer. Her booty was jiggling like two water balloons. It was about twenty degrees in that freezer, but I was sweating.

One night, about two weeks later, she asked me for a ride home after work because her car was in the shop. I was as perfect a gentleman as any man who knew he had a possibility of getting some ass that night would be. I opened her door and, once inside the car, I even offered her some of my weed.

"You smoke?" I asked her while lighting up a big-ass Bob Marley.

"Of course," she purred. We smoked, talked, laughed, and flirted all the way to her house. By the time we got there I was as high as a car note on a brand-new Bentley. Samantha invited me in. "Sorry about the mess," she said before she unlocked the door. I never understood why black people always try and prep you before you go inside their messy-ass house.

As I walked through her place, it was apparent that Samantha came from a broken home. Her TV was broke, her stereo was broke, and looking at all the past due bills on her dining table with a phone book under one leg, I knew Samantha's ass was broke. I couldn't help but think about what one of our coworkers had said about her. D'wayne had said Samantha looked like the girl who lived next door. Yeah? I now thought. If next door was to a crack house.

We went straight to her bedroom. I wasted no time kissing and caressing her. I was hungry for her lips, and my dick was harder than a course in advanced Russian calculus. She started frisking me like I was a shoplifter. I ripped off her clothes and pushed her down on the bed. I then got on top of her, pulled back her ponytail, and took her as hard as I could. A little later, we lay there in her bed, both spent and getting ready for round two.

"How old are you again?" Samantha playfully asked.

"Sixteen," I replied with pride.

"Damn, just a baby. Well, I'm gon' teach yo' ass how to be a sex machine." She paused, seductively biting her full bottom lip. "That's if you want to be my student?"

With a wicked smile, I answered, "This'll be one class I'll never skip. Hell, the semester just started, and I already want extra credit."

Our laughter was interrupted by a knock on the front door. It wasn't a neighborly Can-I-borrow-a-cup-sugar? kind of knock, but a Bam!-Bam!-Bam!-Open-up-this-mother-fucking-door-bitch kind of knock.

"Oh shit, it's Darryl!" she said, jumping out of the bed.

"Who the fuck is Darryl?" I asked nervously but not really wanting to know the answer.

Samantha then said three words a playa never wants to hear: "He's my husband."

"What the—you didn't tell me you were married!" I yelled.

"You never asked, but it's cool, we're separated."

"Then why is he trying to tear down the fucking door?"

She then said the three words that a scared playa absolutely, under any circumstances, never wants to hear: "Because he's kinda crazy."

"How can he be kinda crazy? That's like being kinda broke."

Looking at the dingy ceiling, I became an instant Christian. "Oh God," I prayed, "help me . . . please." All I could think of was what color suit my parents were going to bury me in. I always did look good in black.

The knocks got louder, and so did my heartbeat. I scooped up my clothes and ran into the bathroom. I had one thing on my mind and that was to get . . . the . . . fuck . . . out! I jumped into my pants, stuffed my socks and drawers in my back pockets, and pulled my shirt on backwards—this was way before Kris Kross made it popular.

While Samantha answered the door, I decided to open the bathroom window and make my getaway. I pulled back the shower curtain and was greeted by a black ring around the tub and years of soap scum buildup. I tried to avoid touching anything for fear of getting Ebola. Looking to the window, my heart dropped down to my Converse All Star sneakers.

"Burglar bars?" I mumbled. "What for? She ain't got shit in here to steal." I was royally fucked now. I heard Darryl cursing and slapping Samantha in the living room.

I got mad and started to run to her rescue until I heard Darryl say the four words that any man who is stuck in a bathroom while a jealous and crazy husband is beating the shit out of his wife who is cheating on him with a dude half his age never wants to hear: "I'ma kill that nigga!"

I turned to prayer once again. "Lord, if you get me out of this I swear I'm going to quit getting high, join the first church I see that's open, and then dedicate my life to helping crippled children," I prayed in earnest. Then all of a sudden it got real quiet. Thank the Lord, I thought, God had struck the heathen down. Wrong. Hearing Samantha fall to the floor, I knew the heathen must have struck her down. Sixteen short years of life were passing before my eyes. I could see the headline that would grace tomorrow's newspaper: "Teenager Shot Dead in Nasty Bathroom." I didn't want to go out like that, especially with my clothes on backwards and no drawers on. What would my mother think? The only sound I could hear was my thumping heartbeat and footsteps slowly walking toward the bathroom.

Right then I decided that if I was gon' die, I was gon' die fighting. Frantic, I looked around for a weapon. She didn't have shit in there to fight with, so I grabbed a can of Secret. If Darryl opened the door, I was gonna spray his ass right in the eyes. Armed with the powder blue aerosol can, I was ready for battle. Then I heard a soft knock at the door. I raised the Secret, and I slowly cracked the door open. Much to my surprise and relief, Samantha was at the door. I nervously peeped through the crack.

"I think you better leave."

131

"No shit? What in the fuck do you think I've been trying to do? Where is he?"

"In the kitchen."

"He gon' just let me leave like that?" I felt like a death row inmate who had just been told by the warden that he could walk right out the front gate to freedom.

"Yeah, it's cool." But judging by the big black circles around her eyes, it didn't seem to be cool. She looked like the Hamburglar. Darryl must have been too tired from kicking her ass to want to fight with me. And who was I to argue? I ran out the door like Carl Lewis on crack. I threw her can of Secret on the plastic-covered couch on the way out the door.

"I never hooked up with Samantha again. And that was too bad, because I was looking forward to a full semester of sex ed. But my decision not to see her was based on two things. First, she didn't have a restraining order on crazy-ass Darryl, and the second was that Samantha gave me crabs. But to this day that was the best six minutes of sex I ever had."

Dr. Carter sat stunned. "I don't think that I have told a patient this, but that may have been too much information."

"Crazy, huh? I told you, that stuff seems to always happen to me."

"Stuff like that doesn't just happen. You put yourself in a position for that to happen. In fact, you almost got yourself killed."

"I know that now," LeBaron said, throwing his hands up. "But I didn't know that she was married."

"Put that on your tombstone."

"That's not funny."

"But your choice in women is."

The two made their way to the zoo's exit, then headed in the direction of Dr. Carter's office.

"You said you were army, right?" Dr. Carter said as he threw his empty cup of Coca-Cola into the garbage.

"Yep, three long ass years."

"Have any relationships while you were in?"

"Very few, but the ones I did have were wild."

Dr. Carter smiled. "I may regret this, but let me hear about it."

My grandmother once told me, "LeBaron now, boy, you better be careful what you ask for, because it might just get you." Leave it to Jesse Lee Berry to break out the down-home wisdom. I love the way that old folks twist clichés and sayings around to make a point. And you know what? Their advice is usually right.

I wish my grandmother could have come with me to Germany.

I met Nia on a cold Saturday night at the noncommissioned officers' club. She was talking to a group of women with her back turned to me. And, oh, what a back it was. I walked up behind her and tried to whisper some smooth shit in her ear. I say tried to, because as soon as I breathed into her ear, she jerked around. Now that would have been okay, cause I usually enjoyed startling women, it kept them off balance long enough for me to go in for the kill. But not in this case because when she turned around she had a cigarette in her hand, and it burned me right in the center of my forehead. I had planned to say, "You are the most beautiful woman in here," but instead my first words were, "Bitch, you crazy?"

"Bitch?" she said, rolling her eyes. "You're the bitch sneaking up behind people."

I just shook my head and headed toward the men's room looking like Freddy Krueger. When I walked in the restroom the attendant said, "Damn potna, looks someone put a cigarette out on your forehead."

"No shit, Sherlock," I replied to his astute observation.

I decided then that this was the end of the night for me, but before I left I got a drink to dull the pain, a double Hennessy straight, no chaser. As I made my way out of the club still pissed and slightly lifted, Nia walked up to me and said that she was sorry for using my forehead as an ashtray. Well, not those exact words, but whatever she said, her sweet voice made my head stop hurting. Funny thing how a woman can do that shit to a man.

"Where are you going?" she asked.

"I'm going home."

"Why so early?"

"Because I look like a black Hindu," I said, grinning. The Hennessy was starting to talk for me.

"I think you look cute," she said, the words pouring from her mouth slowly, like syrup.

Boldly I said, "Let's dance." She followed me to the dance floor. The night was back on. We had a blast, my burned forehead and all. After a night of shaking our asses, I knew that it wouldn't be an issue getting those digits. "So, can I call you sometime so that we can do this again?"

"No, you can't," she said in the same syrupy-sweet voice.

I couldn't compute that she had just said no after we'd practically fucked on the dance floor from all the dirty dancing we had done, but I soon understood. She was married.

To many women who were married to soldiers stationed in Germany, the word *marriage* was an obstacle that could be easily overcome. I couldn't count how many of my friends got divorced over there. Everybody was fucking everybody else's wife or husband. Why? It was the fact that many of the husbands had to go in the field for training maneuvers. They could be in the field for as long as ninety days, twice a year. Needless to say, it's hard for a marriage to survive that kind of separation.

Nia's husband was a high-ranking sergeant who spent a lot of time in the field, and he was in the field when I met her. I was surprised by her response, but not put off. The next time I saw her was about two weeks later when she began working at the PX, that's the post's department store. I started shopping there every day. It became part of my daily routine, wake up, brush my teeth, take a shit, shower, then it was off to the PX. At first she rebuffed my advances, but that only made my desire stronger. I prayed to God to just give me one butt-ass-naked night with her. It took me three weeks, but I finally wore her down.

We met at the NCO club again, but this time I told her that it was going to be a smoke-free night. We had a great time. All of my friends were staring at her. To say that she was phat was an understatement. Nia looked like Toni Braxton before Toni Braxton looked like Toni Braxton. I walked her home after we left the club. It was only a few hundred yards away from post housing, so I had to do some quick thinking and talking if I planned on getting in her panties, which was definitely the plan. We walked and talked about all sorts of things, life, love, even the Bible. Yes, the Bible. This woman could quote Scripture better than Billy Graham. Hell, the only Scripture I knew was dinner grace. Is grace a Scripture? Anyway, I didn't feel like talking about religion, but if it would get me inside her temple, I was game.

"LeBaron," she said, "are you spiritual?"

"Hell yeah—I mean, heck yeah. I'm saved, you know?"

"Really?" Nia's eyes lit up. "You go to church?"

"That's where I'm headed after I walk you home." We laughed at my little jokey joke. She laughed like an angel, while my laugh was devilish. By this time we were on her doorstep.

"Would you like to come in for some coffee and a piece of cake?" She innocently batted her eyelids.

Coffee, huh? I interpreted that to mean, Would you like to come in for some coffee and some coochie?

I was all over her from the moment we stepped inside the door. She pushed me off, but not too hard. Kind of like when women say stop all the while letting you take off their clothes? I was so horny I didn't see the pictures of her big-ass husband on the shelf. I sure was glad that he was in the field, because if he could see me grabbing his wife's ass he would have put his big-ass foot in mine.

We sat on the couch. While Nia talked about Bible class, I grabbed her ass. While she tried to catch her breath, I touched her breasts. This went on for nearly an hour. If she had kept that up for much longer, I would've been too tired to have sex. I had never seen a woman who could continue to say "No, stop" while one of her titties was in my mouth. But I was wearing her down. I was an octopus, or better yet, a human pretzel. I had one hand on her zipper, the other on her breast, and one of my legs crossed over hers, while blowing in her ear.

"C'mon baby, I promise it'll be sooo good," I whispered.

"No, I can't, I'm, my hus— Ooh, please stop."

I went into overdrive. "Baby, I'll do it to you so good, you'll want to give me a tip."

We went back and forth.

"No."

"Yes."

"I can't."

"You can."

Twenty more minutes went by, and I was glad that I had eaten my Wheaties for breakfast.

After an hour and a half of wrestling, I had her top off, bra undone, and pants around her ankles. I continued boasting about how I was going to crack her back if she would just let me. And then all of a sudden she let go. I didn't realize it at first, but Nia wasn't resisting anymore. I thought that I'd given the girl a stroke. "Are you all right?" I asked, pulling back.

She just stared at me for about five seconds and then said, "You really want to fuck me, huh?"

"More than poor kids want Christmas presents," I said with a sly grin.

"Will you fuck me hard and long?" she purred.

"What the hell?" I thought. Who was this talking dirty to me? Because it damn sure wasn't the nun I came in there with.

"LeBaron," she whispered, "are you going to fuck the shit out of me?"

I gulped, but all of a sudden my throat was dry. "Uh ... yeah ... I ... am ... going ... to ... fuck ... the ... shit ... out ... of ... you?" It came out more like a question than a statement.

"Good." She stood up and pulled off her panties. She turned around and grabbed her ankles. "Then come over here and fuck this bitch, you black motherfucker."

"Oh shit!" I said under my breath.

"C'mon, nigga," she commanded in a husky voice. "Quit bullshittin' and come fuck me."

My dick went from hard as a rock to soft as cotton candy. When I didn't move, Nia turned around and noticed my limpness.

"Oh hell naw, motherfucker! You wanted to fuck, so we're gonna fuck. Gimme that dick." Nia got on her knees and proceeded to give me the best head I ever had. I swear I saw birds and stars and shit floating around my head like in the cartoons. I was soon hard again, but my knees were shaking like asses on lap dancers. Nia got up off her knees, turned back around and grabbed her ankles again. I wished she'd stop doing that, because it made me nervous. She had scared the hell out of me. I felt like a thirteen-year-old. My heart pounded in my chest, and, although it was the dead of winter, I was sweating like a black man at a Klan rally.

I got behind her and eased my way inside. She felt good. She moaned, I moaned. But Nia was moaning because she was just getting going, I moaned because I was coming. "Oh God, no," I prayed. "Please make it stop, or go back in, do something," but it was too late. After just eight good, strong strokes, my well was dry.

She turned around and said, "Don't tell me you came?"

"OK," I said, "I won't tell you."

She rose up and looked at me pitifully and said, "You know you ain't never getting this pussy again, right?"

I nodded my head like a child and said, "Yes, ma'am." I

was so embarrassed. I tried to leave, but Nia ordered me to sit down.

"LeBaron," she said, "one of the biggest problems with men is that most of y'all are too damn impatient. You guys are just like little boys at Christmas. You beg and plead for a certain present but after you get it, you play with it for a while then throw it in the closet. And y'all grow up and treat women like presents. Well, a woman damn sure ain't no toy, and my pussy ain't nothing to be played with. That's my soul, my being. And I'm telling you, my pussy is worth more than five minutes of some bullshit-ass sex."

I felt about five inches tall. "But—"

"But my ass," she cut me off. "You have to first make love to a woman's mind and then learn her body. Learn her likes and dislikes, how and where she likes to be kissed and why. And calm the fuck down; if you can't swim, why would you jump off into the deep end of the pool? That's why your ass drowned."

"Nia was true to her word. I never again saw any parts of her pussy. But she did leave me with something to remember her by: her words and this big-ass scar on my forehead."

"That was one crazy story." Dr. Carter laughed. "But we all got one."

LeBaron patted Dr. Carter on the back and said. "Well then, tell me yours."

Dr. Carter enjoyed another hearty laugh. "I think not. LeBaron, you are something else. You should write a book."

"You think? But who would buy a book about my experiences?"

"Shakespeare once asked that question. One thing is certain, those experiences were definitely lust."

Laughing in agreement, LeBaron said, "I guess I've fallen victim to lust most of the time."

"I couldn't have said it better myself," Dr. Carter said. He smiled as confusion crept across LeBaron's face. "That's right, you just nailed it."

"Nailed what?"

"That a man can never fulfill his potential until he can control lust. The sexual urge is one of the strongest forces known. Few men or women can resist its siren song. It's like a drug; it clouds and confuses the mind. You can make some of the worst decisions in life while high on lust."

"Ain't that the truth," LeBaron said. "It's interesting, since I've been coming to see you I have gone over most of my relationships before Phoenix, and she's the only one who I wanted for more than sex. All the other women I've loved or, I should say, lusted after, were just about sex and a pretty face."

"You're right. And if you only follow your animal instinct without using the logic of your brain, do you know what will happen?" LeBaron thought for a moment but could only stare blankly at Dr. Carter. "I'll tell you what happens, you'll only end up getting fucked."

LeBaron felt like Plato sitting at the feet of Socrates. It amazed him the way Dr. Carter explained complex topics in a layman's terms. "But you have to admit that the urge for sex is kind of hard to ignore."

"It's impossible to ignore. The only way to truly overcome it is by understanding your purpose and being disciplined enough to stay true to it. Remember when I told you of woman's divine purpose?"

"How could I forget."

"Well we have one too, an equally important one. The responsibility of the earth and all of the life on it rests on our shoulders. Just like the lion, we must protect our pride. We are entrusted with the awesome task of sustaining life and guarding the world. Sadly, we have fucked up both of our tasks. We've spoiled our rivers and seas, destroyed our forests and croplands, and we are poisoning the very air we breathe. The earth is more than four billion years old, and we've managed to nearly destroy her in less than a few hundred years. And at the same time we've destroyed our relationships and poisoned a generation of young boys and girls."

"But when is it going to stop?" LeBaron asked.

Dr. Carter paused briefly before answering, "When each man accepts his destiny as the guardian of life. However, he will never realize that until he stops falling victim to what he lusts after."

Chapter Seventeen

"I could get used to Paris," Phoenix said aloud, admiring her reflection in the bathroom mirror. "And I could definitely get used to Chance." She glanced at her watch. "Damn, I better hurry up, I'm late."

Fashion Week was turning out to be everything Phoenix had hoped for and more. Maxine had introduced her to many of the top designers and models, including Naomi Campbell, Phoenix's favorite. Naomi had even said that with Phoenix's good looks and figure she should try modeling. Phoenix blushed for a day after that compliment. She was a million miles away from D.C. and loving it. But by far, the best part of the trip had been her evenings with Chance. Each day had been the same, yet different. Chance would take her sightseeing in the morning, runway watching in the afternoon and dancing at night. One night stood out in particular. They'd been heading to the Wax Club, a disco that had incredibly lifelike wax replicas of famous people, including a Michael Jordan statue that was especially lifelike. The club was located in the heart of Paris's red-light district. All along the sidewalk were doorways leading into bordellos with prostitutes standing in the doorways wearing sheer teddies or just a bra and thong. Phoenix shook her head in amazement as she relived the night in her mind.

"Phoenix?" Chance had said, grinning. "Look at all these hookers hanging out, this shit is crazy."

"You mean, letting it all hang out." Phoenix had blushed, clutching his arm tighter. "These women have no shame."

"But they got plenty of ass," Chance had said, laughing at his own joke. "Hey, did you know prostitutes have contributed a lot to the fashion industry." Phoenix had stopped walking.

"What?" she'd said, staring at him.

"Yeah, that lipstick you're wearing, you know that comes from ancient prostitutes?"

"Whatever," Phoenix had frowned. "How so?"

"Serious business, Phoenix, I saw it on the History Channel. Back in ancient times when a whore specialized in oral sex, she'd paint her lips red and stand outside her place of business to advertise."

"Get outta here!" Phoenix had laughed in disbelief. "That isn't true."

"Oh yes it is," he'd said, holding her tight. "And I noticed something about you too."

"What's that, baby?" she'd playfully asked.

"You wear a lot of lipstick."

Phoenix had pushed him away and given him her best "ghetto girl" headshake. "Well, don't think I'll be tasting any ancient history tonight." She'd then fallen into his arms, both of them laughing.

Phoenix was having a ball, and thanks to Maxine, she and Chance got invited to all the exclusive parties. They made quite the handsome couple, attracting stares whenever they walked into a room. He was the consummate escort, and even though he was always surrounded by a bevy of beautiful women, his eyes never left Phoenix. Tonight, they were going to the Christian Dior party, and Phoenix was already running fifteen minutes late. She twisted the shower's knob to hot, and steam quickly filled the bathroom. She smiled to herself, thoughts of Chance filling her head once again. Although he was tall, gorgeous, intelligent and successful, he wasn't stuck on himself like most of the other pretty boy models at the shows. Furthermore, he was heterosexual, which was a definite plus. He'd been a gentleman the entire week, never once trying to spend the night with her. After a night's partying they usually ended up walking along the Champs-Elysées, where she'd go on and on about LeBaron. Sometimes she'd cry and Chance would envelop her in the warmth of his arms and listen. While careful not to be the victim of a European fling, Phoenix couldn't help but think of Chance.

As the hot water hit her naked flesh, Phoenix fantasized that her soapy hands were replaced by Chance's. She thought of his tattoo, two crossed spears over a Zulu shield, which he had over his heart. Yesterday, while they'd been sitting in a lounge chair on his room's private balcony, she'd asked him to take off his shirt so that she could see it. Chance had been only too happy to oblige her. The tattoo was in honor of his ancestors who were Zulu warriors. He'd proudly told her of how his family could trace their roots back past slavery. The story had turned her on when she'd reached out to trace the tattoo with her fingertips. Her breathing had slowed as she'd tenderly outlined the shield. Without giving it a thought, Chance had put one hand over Phoenix's and, with the other, pulled her into him, kissing her lightly on her lips. Phoenix hadn't been able to resist him and had nearly jumped into his arms, kissing him like he was a soldier going off to war. Turning around, she'd wrapped his muscular arms around her waist. She'd giggled as he'd nibbled on her earlobe. He'd begun massaging her slender shoulders while he'd kissed her nape. Phoenix had been lost in the passion of Paris, the mood of the moon, and the charms of Chance. But she hadn't been that lost, because she hadn't given in to temptation and had soon gone back to her room. "Yeah," she thought now, stepping out of the shower, "it would take more than a few moonlit walks and some innocent kissing to get me in bed, no matter how well-developed his pectorals are."

Chapter Eighteen

"It's stuffy in here, I need to light an incense," LeBaron mumbled after unlocking his office door and walking inside. His office was just as he had left it a week ago, nicely decorated and the envy of the other managers. The desk was clean and all the items on it neatly organized. Unlike the posters that adorned the other offices, his prints were black art. Little black figurines and African statues were carefully placed around a framed picture of a black Jesus that sat on a mahogany shelf. Lamps placed in three corners of the office gave off a soft light that reflected nicely off a framed picture of Phoenix and his two dark green ferns. LeBaron felt good to finally be back at work. Throughout the day people stopped by his office to welcome him back. They commented on how well he looked considering that he'd had the flu or whatever Eric had told them he'd had. LeBaron looked rested and felt rejuvenated.

The sessions with Dr. Carter were making him more comfortable with himself. He was beginning to understand the divine role of man and woman.

"What a fool I've been," he said to himself, staring at Phoenix's picture.

"What's up?" Eric said, popping his head into the office.

LeBaron jumped back. "Damn, you scared the shit out of me."

"Glad to see your ass is back among the living." Eric walked in and gave LeBaron a pound.

"Thanks, man, good to be back, and thanks for covering for me."

"No sweat, you know I'm an excellent liar."

"Yeah, me and all your ex-girlfriends."

"Whatever, anyway I stopped by to make sure you'll be at my birthday party tonight. I know you've been getting all spiritual and shit lately."

"Enlightened, my brother, that's all," LeBaron said, pointing his finger toward the ceiling. "You know I'll be there."

"Good," Eric winked. " 'Cause I got a surprise for you."

Later that evening LeBaron headed out to Club Dreams. It was the District's newest watering hole for black professionals. Located on 7th Street just off New York Avenue, the restaurant and bar's classy, quiet and reserved atmosphere was an alternative to the area's usual weekend meat markets. But on this night, the place was loud and packed with people. It was rented out for Eric's birthday party. On hand were a few professional ball players from the Redskins and Wizards, local television personalities, and members of D.C.'s buppie set. And what birthday party for Eric would be complete without hoochies? And there were plenty of them on this night. LeBaron's eyes burned from the cigar smoke, cheap cologne and perfume. As he looked around the room he smiled, but it was a smile of pity. He felt as if he knew something that everyone else there didn't. His desire to be single and mingle was definitely on the wane, but he couldn't let his boy down on his birthday. LeBaron walked outside to the balcony to get some fresh air. Sipping his customary Rémy Martin, he reflected on the past week.

It had been mentally and emotionally tough but also refreshing. He thought of a phrase that Dr. Carter had said: "Before a sword is truly a sword, it must first be burned, hammered, and pounded into shape." Yeah, a sword, that's what he felt like.

"Hey, bruh," Eric said, walking out onto the balcony. "So this is where you're hiding. I've been looking all over for you."

"What's up, birthday boy?"

"Just chilling, but look at who I found." Eric stepped aside to reveal a sight that LeBaron had never wanted to see again in his life. He almost dropped his glass when the long-legged beauty stepped forward.

"Hello, LeBaron," she said, wrapping her arms around his neck and kissing him on the cheek.

"India?" LeBaron managed to say, standing there stiffly.

"Well, I'll let you two lovebirds get reacquainted," Eric said, then walked back into the party.

They stood there a long time just staring at each other. India broke the awkward silence. "It's been a long time, L."

"Yeah, four years, two months and seven days," he snapped. "But who's counting?"

"You, obviously," she sucked her teeth and frowned.

"I see you still have that quick tongue."

She put her hands on her hips. "You used to like that quick tongue."

"Used to, as in past tense," he sharply reminded her. LeBaron paused three seconds for effect. "Anyways, India, what have you been doing with yourself? Did you pass the bar?"

"Yes, I've been working with the L.A. public defender's office for the past three years."

"Congratulations."

"Thanks, I hear you're a big-shot TV executive now."

"I wouldn't say big shot."

Smiling, she said, "That's my L, always modest."

"What brings you to town, vacation?"

"No, relocation."

"Huh?" LeBaron said while nearly spitting out his drink.

"I'm moving back to join my uncle Walter's law firm."

"But I thought you didn't want to stay here? I thought you wanted to find your fortune on the West Coast? If I recall correctly, that was the reason why you left me."

"I know, I know, but Los Angeles wasn't all sunshine and beaches. Too many gangbanging clients and superficial Hollywood types can take their toll on the soul. Besides, my uncle needs help with his firm." She paused and stepped up on LeBaron once again. Her firm breasts brushed against his chest. "Plus, I also have some unfinished business here."

"Oh really?" LeBaron said casually, although his heart was thumping like a Dr. Dre and Snoop track. "And what business is that?"

"Don't be silly. You know I'm talking about us." LeBaron stood there speechless. He gulped his drink, but his throat was still dry. India ran her hand slowly down his arm and grasped his hand. With a slight tug, she said, "So L, you wanna get out of here?"

Chapter Nineteen

For years Dr. Carter's Georgetown town house had served as the setting for his many affairs. But since his three-month separation from his wife, it had become his permanent residence. The Tudor-style home looked right out of the pages of *Architectural Digest*. Expensive hand-woven rugs lay on the polished hardwood floors. Exotic antiques adorned every room: his favorite was the den, where oak and mahogany accents accompanied leather furniture. The fireplace gave a warm glow to the muted décor.

Staring at the fire, it was hard for him not to compare the flames to what was happening to him right now. His sessions with LeBaron were igniting and rekindling his passion for his profession. He stood up from the couch and walked over to the bar, where he poured himself a tumbler of scotch. Sipping it slowly, he stared at his beautiful protégée lounging on the leather couch dressed in a short pink-and-blue silk robe.

"I really think LeBaron is the patient I've been looking for."

"I can tell that a change has come over you," Angela said.

"He has renewed my interest in my work. And after only a few sessions, I really think he's making progress."

"If I may ask," she said, "what's his problem?"

Leighton walked over to the fireplace and stared into the flames. "In an attempt to uphold doctor-patient confidentiality, let me just say that his problem is the same three problems all men have."

"And what are they, sweetheart?"

"Dishonesty, fear of commitment, and a lust to fuck everything in sight," Leighton said as he drank the last of the warm scotch from his glass.

Angela stood, allowing the throw pillows covering her legs to fall to the floor. Her oiled legs glistened in the firelight. The sight made Leighton glad that he was a man. She put her hands around his waist and hugged him tight. In her eyes he saw a confidence never seen before.

"Leighton, mind if I ask you a question?"

"Of course not, sweetheart, my life is an open book for you."

Clearing her throat, she said, "How is it that you can give this great advice on relationships to people and at the same time—"

"And at the same time be in the midst of an affair with a woman twenty-five years younger than myself?"

"Well, yeah."

"Angela, baby, I struggle with the same demons as my patients. Sometimes I win, and sometimes I lose."

"Leighton, that's a cop-out," she said in exasperation. "I hate it when men say shit like that."

"You're right, Angela. I am a hypocrite and the biggest one of all, because I know better. The reason I do what I do is the same reason as other men, because I am weak. But I am too old for this shit—I understand that now. I feel like a fool counseling others when my own personal life is in the toilet."

"Nobody's perfect, Leighton."

"I know we all have problems, but think of how much easier life would be if we eliminated the problems we caused ourselves?"

"I agree," she said, clearing her throat. "Leighton, I know that now is not the perfect time to say this, but—"

He pressed his fingers to her lips to silence her. "Angela, I know." He stared into her wide brown eyes. "There is no need to say what we both know."

"I'll always love you," she said, tears moistening her cheeks.

He held her close and whispered, "I'll treasure our moments together forever." Leighton released Angela from his embrace. She disappeared upstairs and returned minutes later fully dressed. Leighton was waiting by the door when she came downstairs. "If you ever need anything, don't hesitate to call me."

"I won't," she said, holding his hands. He watched her walk to her car. She waved, he waved, and then she drove off in her little red Mazda Miata. They both knew they would never see each other again. He poured another drink and thought how strange life could be. In the span of fifteen minutes his life had changed three times. He'd found his passion, lost his mistress, and gained back his soul. But there was one more thing he had to get back. He hesitated at first, but he reached for the phone and dialed the numbers that he'd committed to memory so long ago.

"Hello?" the weary voice on the other end said.

"Tina, I'm ready to come home."

Her heart sank at the sound of his voice. It had been three long, lonely months without him. After composing herself, she whispered, "I'll leave the light on."

Chapter Twenty

"Chance, yet again I've had a wonderful evening," Phoenix said, standing in the doorway of her hotel room.

"Me too," he said, inching closer. He gently kissed her bottom lip. "But I'm not ready for it to end. Can't I come in for a little nightcap?"

Phoenix felt powerless against his charms. Her resistance was quickly waning, but she held on to her resolve. "No, Chance, I think we've had enough fun for one night."

"Please," he said, bending to one knee. "I'll beg."

Phoenix giggled at the sight of an international supermodel on bended knee at her feet. His smile disarmed her and turned her on immensely. "Um . . . OK . . . but just one drink."

"Just one drink, I promise." He rose to his feet and walked through her door.

*   *   *

"Shit!" LeBaron mumbled while fumbling with the keys, trying to unlock India's apartment door. Until she found her own place, India was living at the Pennsylvania House, an exclusive building of furnished apartments in Northwest D.C. She stood behind LeBaron, her arms wrapped around his waist, playfully caressing his chest.

"Do you need some help finding the hole?"

"Uh, nah, there it is, I got it," LeBaron said as the lock clicked and the door gave way. "Nice place you have here, the law must be treating you well." LeBaron attempted light conversation.

"It's OK, I suppose," she said, lounging on the plush cream-colored love seat. LeBaron sat in a chair across the room. "Why are you sitting so far away from me?" she purred. "Come closer. I won't bite. I might nibble, but I won't bite."

LeBaron reluctantly got up to sit next to India. He knew from the moment he'd agreed to leave the party that he'd made a mistake. Going home with India was the last thing he should have done, but she was a hard woman to resist.

India moved closer to LeBaron and started rubbing the back of his neck with her fingertips. "L, I'm so sorry about what happened between us, but I was young and stubborn. I had to get L.A. out of my system."

"It's cool, India." LeBaron tried to concentrate as he was getting increasingly turned on. "We all make mistakes, but you can't just expect to come back into my life. Things are different now."

"What's different? I know all about what happened with Phoenix. Eric told me everything."

"Oh he did, did he? What did he tell you?"

"Well, for one he told me that she dumped you."

"She didn't dump me."

"OK, well she broke up with you."

"But we're still working on things."

"How so? Eric says she's out of the country."

"She's coming back in a few days."

"Why do you want to waste your time on her? She left you."

"And so did you."

"But I'm different."

"How?"

"You love me."

"Correction, I loved you. I love her."

India stood in front of LeBaron in order to get his full attention. "C'mon, L, I see it in your eyes that you want me. You know we were meant to be together. Remember the love we used to make?" India began unbuttoning her blouse.

"That was a long time ago," LeBaron said while trying not to look. She unzipped her skirt, letting it and her blouse fall to the floor.

Damn, LeBaron thought. *She's still finer than a motherfucker.* Swallowing hard, he managed to say, "Now why are you doing that?"

She stepped out of her clothes and walked over to dim

the lights. She turned around to light a candle, just enough for him to see her red thong. India felt his eyes burning a mark onto her ass. "You know, you could get thirty days in jail in some states for what you are thinking of doing right now."

Yeah, he thought, *but it would be worth it.*

The candle sufficiently lit, she turned her attentions to LeBaron, who sat rigid on the love seat. She stood in front of him and climbed onto his lap, straddling him. "Mmm . . . I can feel that you missed me," she whispered.

LeBaron's breathing was heavy. Undoing the buttons of his shirt, India slid her hands inside and squeezed his nipples. " I really missed you," India said while grinding her hips into LeBaron's pelvis. That did it. LeBaron grabbed the back of her neck and kissed her like a soldier who had just come back from war. His hungry hands traveled all over her body. She drew back and unhooked her bra. Her breasts beckoned for him to take them into his mouth.

"LeBaron, I want you to fuck me. Right here, right now." India rolled off LeBaron and rested back on the love seat. She eased her panties down and spread her legs. "I know you remember how good this pussy is."

Beads of sweat formed on his forehead.

"Well?" India asked impatiently.

"Uh . . . yeah," he replied. "But I have to get a condom."

"That's OK baby, I trust you."

"No way. I have one in my gym bag in my car. I'll be right back." LeBaron stood and buttoned his shirt.

"Hurry up, OK. You don't want me to catch cold."

"A woman as hot as you could never get cold," LeBaron said, grabbing his keys. Although his car was parked right outside the complex, it took him forever to reach it. He felt like a condemned prisoner walking to the electric chair. He reached the car and dropped his keys two times before finally unlocking the door. He sat in the driver's seat with the door open and one leg outside on the pavement. He reached over into the backseat, grabbed his gym bag, and pulled the condoms out. When he turned back around, his ragged reflection stared back at him in the rearview mirror.

How can I do this? he thought. *How can I have sex with India? But damn, she is gorgeous and sexy and she wants me. Who would know? It could be our secret. One last piece won't hurt. It won't hurt her, but what about me? I don't want her. I want Phoenix. Dr. Carter is right—"A man can never be in control of himself until he conquers his lust." Are a few hours of pleasure worth it?*

"Hell no!"

LeBaron pulled his leg inside the car and slammed the door shut. He put his key in the ignition and started the car. His tires screeched as he turned into traffic. Rolling down his window, a burst of cool air greeted him before he threw the condoms into the street.

* * *

So much for the nightcap, Phoenix thought. She felt like she belonged in Chance's strong arms. After carrying her to the bed, he began gently caressing her shoulders, then kissing her lips and neck.

"Oh, Phoenix, I want you so bad."

"I want you too, Chance."

He kissed her hungrily while unbuttoning her blouse. He met with no resistance. She helped him out of his shirt and ran her fingers across his powerful chest, then kissed his neck. "You like that?" she said.

"That feels so good." He lay back on the bed and rolled her on top of him. He cupped her ass cheeks with his large hands and squeezed.

"Oh," Phoenix sang. He rolled her over onto her back and started kissing her breasts. Passion and pleasure washed over Phoenix as she closed her eyes and arched her back.

Chance rose and began to take off his shirt and unbuckle his belt. "Can I make love to you, Phoenix?"

"Make love to me, LeBaron." The words left her mouth, and Chance's body went limp. Phoenix immediately realized her error and burst into tears. "Oh my God, Chance! I'm so sorry. I can't do this."

Chance sat on the edge of the bed. Phoenix sat up and covered her chest with her arms and what was left of her blouse.

"I'm still in love with LeBaron. I just can't, Chance. I just can't. I'm sorry," Phoenix sobbed.

Chance hung his head and ran his hands over his hair.

"I understand. I guess love is just a little bit stronger than lust."

"Do you really understand? Are you mad?"

"No, I'm not mad. I'm disappointed but not mad. I couldn't look at myself in the mirror if we were together and you were still in love with him."

"Chance," she said, kissing him on the cheek, "you're so sweet."

"Yeah, that's me, Sweet Chance."

"Don't worry, you'll find the one for you."

"I guess. I should leave now."

Phoenix walked him to the door, but before he left she hugged him real tight. "Chance, I know this might sound strange, but thank you."

With glassy eyes he looked into hers and could only manage to say, "You're welcome." Phoenix closed the door, walked to the bed, climbed back in, and cried herself to sleep.

Chapter Twenty-one

"Hello, Dr. Carter's office. Oh sure, LeBaron, come on up."
Dr. Carter smiled. He couldn't remember the last time he had
answered his own office phone. There had always been someone there to do it and to run interference. But now that Angela
had resigned, he was on his own, at least until he could find a
temp. This time he'd hire a fat and ugly one. Meanwhile, he'd
enjoy answering the phone. It was a great way to connect with
his patients. "That's what it was all about," he reflected; his
sessions with LeBaron were proving it.

LeBaron didn't know it as he walked into the office, but
this was to be his last session. Dr. Carter instinctively knew
when his patients were ready to face their demons, and
LeBaron was more than ready, he could feel it.

"Hey, Leighton, how ya' doing?"

"I'm doing quite well, but I think it is I who should be
asking you that question."

"I'm great, and you are going to be so proud of me, I resisted a great temptation a few nights ago."

"Oh, really? Tell me about it."

"It was an old girlfriend, India. I was so in love with her."

"Good for you, but who is this lady? You neglected to tell me about her."

LeBaron cleared his throat. "It was a bad deal, Leighton, I don't know if I can talk about her."

Dr. Carter was silent.

"OK, India was the first woman I actually wanted to marry. In fact, I did propose to her."

"And?" Dr. Carter said in a serious tone, at the same time scribbling on his legal pad.

I met India Piahno in the summer of '95. I was living in New York City and working at WNBC, the NBC network's local news station. I produced the wildly popular *Live at Five* newscasts. The shows were a mix of news, entertainment and the off-the-wall antics of my anchors Chuck Scarborough, Sue Simmons and Al Roker, who was also doing double duty as the weatherman on the *Today* show. They were three legends of the New York media and also great to work with. They all earned more than a couple of million dollars each a year, and in the hyperkinetic and ultrastress-filled industry known as local news, were known as the gold standard.

It was an exciting time and place for a twenty-six-year-old producer. I revolved in a circle most people dream of. Working at the famous 30 Rockefeller Plaza, you were liable to meet all types of celebrities. Our newsroom was on the seventh floor, the same floor where *Saturday Night Live* is taped. Our control room and set were on the sixth floor, right across the hall from where *The Conan O'Brien Show* is taped. Man, in the hallway you might see Madonna, Tom Brokaw, dancing monkeys or even baby elephants dropping adult-sized shit all over the place. I even met Chris Rock in the men's room one day. I nearly pissed on him trying to shake his hand. Those were crazy times.

India was interning as my production assistant. She would print my show scripts, research stories and basically do whatever I didn't have time to do. She was attending NYU Law School, and the internship was a requirement for her Communications Law course.

I love being around smart and beautiful women, and India was definitely smart and beautiful, so we hit it off immediately. Maybe too well, because after a few weeks of working together, our working relationship morphed into some old cosmic codependent shit. If I didn't speak to her as soon as I got to work, she'd act all pissy with me. I couldn't even talk about other women without her getting jealous. Not crazy jealous, but she had that look that women give you which said, "I don't want to hear about that bitch." I have to admit too that when the guys in the office would talk about how fine India was, I'd get a little peeved. I couldn't figure why I was so drawn to her. I mean she was twenty-one years old! I'd never been attracted to younger women before. They bored me, but not India. She was well read and I'm not talking 'bout that sistergirl-brotherman shit, I'm talking serious books. She quoted passages from Baltasar Gracián as well as Machiavelli.

Now, even with all of her good looks and brains, India was self-conscious about her upbringing. She grew up poor on Sound Beach, Long Island, about two and a half hours from Manhattan. It was a small town filled with Italian, goodfella guido-ass muthafuckas. Her mother, Annabella, was a dark Sicilian, and her father, who had been run off by the guidos, was Buckwheat black, so you know she caught shit growing up. To pay for community college and now law school, her mother worked two jobs while India worked part-time at Tristan's, an upscale and trendy clothing store across the street from Rockefeller Plaza. She was the second person in her family to graduate from college, the first being an uncle who had a small struggling law practice in D.C. I think part of her attraction to me was that she thought I was rich. It was no secret at the station that producers made more than a hundred thousand dollars a year, and to a poor kid from L.I., that might as well have been a million dollars.

After about a month, it was clear that we were attracted to each other, but neither of us would admit it or act on it. I was ready for this charade to come to an end, so I decided to find out just how much she liked me. Over the weeks she'd interned I'd learned that she loved her some Prince. She had all of his CDs and she'd mentioned that she some-times wore purple thongs in his honor. I squeezed many a bottle of cocoa butter fantasizing about her wearing them. So part one began . . . Through a ticket scalper friend of mine, I managed to get two tickets to Prince's upcoming concert at Madison Square Garden. The concert was on a Friday, and I sprung the news on her the Monday before.

"What's up, LeBaron?" India said, while she dropped her purse on her desk, which was next to mine.

I faked a grimace and said, "I got problems, girl."

"What's wrong?" she said as she stepped closer to my desk.

"I don't want to even trouble you." I shrugged and sighed heavily, flexing my acting skills.

"Boy, you better tell me what's wrong," she said with her sassy Long Island attitude that I loved.

"OK, if you must know," I said shaking my head. "I have two tickets to the Prince concert on Friday at the Garden and I don't have anybody to go with."

"What!" India screamed. "You got what? Prince tickets?"

I raised my hands in mock surrender. "Damn girl, calm down."

"I'm going to that concert with you, LeBaron."

"Are you asking me or telling me?" I smirked.

"Telling you."

"Well, since you said it so nice, I guess we are going to the Garden."

"It's a date," she gushed.

No. It's about to be on.

By Friday morning, I had come up with a satisfactory plan to seduce India. I put part two into action as soon as I got to work. "Hey India, ready for the concert?"

"Ready? I couldn't even sleep last night," she said. She had some clothes she'd just picked up from the cleaners, and she hung them up on a wall hook.

"Couldn't sleep? C'mon," I said with an incredulous look. "You act like you've never been to a concert before."

"I haven't," she said, the smile disappearing from her face.

"What! You've got be kidding?"

"Nope." She shook her head and looked at the floor.

"Well then, we are going to do it up tonight."

"Really?" Her face brightened again. "What you got planned?"

"First, we go to the concert."

"What else?" she demanded impatiently.

"Then we'll go dancing at Nell's."

"Nell's? I've never been there but I've heard it's really nice. Hey, where're your clothes?" she asked, looking around the room. "Are you wearing what you have on to the concert?"

"No, sweetheart, my clothes are at the hotel."

"Hotel?" she said.

"Yeah, whenever I go out in the city I always get a suite at the Plaza 50, 'cause I know I won't be in any shape to drive back to Harlem."

Her eyebrows shot upward. "Damn, I was going to get ready here."

"Well, you're more than welcome to shower and change at the hotel. It has two full bathrooms," I offered, sincerity dripping from my voice.

"Great!" She hugged me, then went about her work for the day.

I smiled as I watched her bounce away. "How great it's going to be to see your ass buck naked!"

India was impressed as the driver opened the back door of the black Lincoln Town Car later that night. "Oh my," she said, sliding her shapely body into the backseat. "I see we're riding in style tonight."

I smiled. "You didn't think I'd take you to a Prince concert in a yellow cab, did ya?"

"Mr. Brown, you certainly know how to treat a lady."

"Nothing but the best for the best, Miss Piahno."

After a fifteen-minute drive to Madison Square Garden, we arrived forty-five minutes early to a packed Garden. Black people definitely knew how to dress for a night out on the town. But many of them were better suited for going out in the country. "Now look at that," I said, directing India's attention to a brother in a red suit complete with red alligator shoes. "They got some country-ass niggas in New York City."

"Ooh, look LeBaron, what about her? She should be ashamed of herself," India said, pointing to a sister with a big rhinoceros ass that was stretching the hell out of a tan catsuit with holes running up her legs and arms. It was so tight you could hear the threads screaming for mercy.

All I could do was shake my head. "Damn, I thought Prince was playing tonight, not Shabba Ranks."

"Shabba!" we said in unison, laughing.

Our seats were great. We were to the left of the stage with a perfect view. India nearly fainted when Prince rose from a trapdoor in the stage. His highness was wearing a tight-assed white silk shirt and pants. Around my way we called pants like that hug-a-nuts. But I had to admit Prince was the only nigga I know who could look cool in that shit, not to mention the white leather high-heeled boots. His show was awesome, for two hours he sang his biggest hits. As India mouthed the words to "Do Me Baby," I couldn't help but think that I planned to do just that in a few more hours.

Our next stop was Nell's, and when we got there the line was around the corner. The velvet rope was in full effect, but not for us. One of my good friends was working the door, and he let us walk right in. Once again, India was impressed. I felt like the man as the confused people in the line wondered what made us so special.

"Uh-huh," I said, nudging India toward the dance floor, "your ass been bragging all week about how well you can dance. Let's see what kind of skills you got."

"Boy, you ain't said nothing but a word, let's do it."

And we damn near did. India was grinding me like a sack of Starbucks coffee beans. My dick was harder than a black man trying to qualify for a mortgage. I tried to play it off, but I couldn't. The teepee rising from my crotch gave me away. Every time India would turn around and grind her ass up against me, I poked her. "Ooh, what's that?" she said, grinning.

"That's just Russell."

"Russell?"

"Yeah, Russell the love muscle."

She laughed so hard she stopped dancing. "Love muscle, huh? Well, it looks like Russell's on steroids."

"Nah baby, all protein," I deadpanned.

After two hours of drinking, dancing and sweating the starch out of our outfits, we were both eager to leave. It was nearly 2 A.M. when the Lincoln dropped us off at the hotel.

"Damn, it's two in the morning," India frowned, looking at her watch. "Shit, the last train left at one-thirty." Inwardly, I smiled. Everything was going according to plan.

"Really?" I said with mock concern. "I thought they ran all night?"

"Nah, the last one is gone."

I was silent as we rode the elevator up to my suite. I had the upper hand now—in fact, I was holding all spades. She broke the silence. "Umm . . . LeBaron, do you mind if I stay here?"

"Of course not," I said nonchalantly. "Mi casa es su casa." Bam! Ace of spades.

"Thank you," she said as I unlocked the door.

I waved her off. "No prob, I'll sleep on the couch." Bam! Little Joker.

"No, no," she pleaded. "It's your suite. We'll both sleep in the bed. I mean, if you don't mind?"

"I don't care," I lied. "It doesn't matter to me." But in reality nothing on earth mattered as much to me.

"OK, it's settled, let's go to bed," she said, jumping on the queen-sized bed. Bam! Big Joker and her ass was set.

I smiled and began to undress. I was wearing my good drawers. You know those clean-just-in-case-you-get-into-a-car-accident drawers? They were my lucky white silk boxers with little red lips stamped all over them.

"Nice underoos," India said, making no attempt to hide her smile.

"Don't joke," I said, tucking both thumbs in the waist-band. "These shorts have been around the world."

"You can say that again," she frowned.

"Oh? Well, let's see yours."

She pulled off her short and very tight black En Vogue look-alike dress to reveal a purple push-up bra and match-ing thong that her ass absolutely swallowed. India's ass made my head hurt, both of them. She did a pirouette. "Well? What do you think?"

"I can't."

"Can't what?"

"Think."

"Boy, you're so corny," she said, turning off the lamp.

Nah, me so horny, I thought as my hand nearly choked Russell to death.

"And don't be getting all fresh either," she said, reaching over to love tap me while I couldn't wait to love tap that ass.

"Whatever, girl," I said, because actually what I had in mind wasn't fresh at all, in fact it was quite stanky.

As soon as the lamp was turned off, a lightbulb turned on in my head. "How can I get this ass?" I mused while staring at the ceiling. India turned her back and scooted her ass right next to my hip and fell asleep almost immediately. Not me, I was wide awake like I was on guard duty. And I was, I was guarding the booty.

OK, I thought, *if I turn and brush my dick up against her ass and she doesn't trip, it's on.* I turned halfway over and she didn't move away. *Cool*, I thought, *now if I could just swing my left arm over and rest my hand ever so slightly under her left titty.*

"Boy, what you doing?" she mumbled, interrupting my devious thoughts.

"If you got to ask, then I must not be doing it right," I mumbled right back.

"What you said?"

"Just trying to get comfortable, that's all."

"Oh, OK," she said, turning her back to me once again.

Damn, I was back to square one. I waited for about five minutes, then launched phase two. Shit, this was war. I brushed my left hand ever so gently on her plump ass. I uncurled my fingers, then began to lightly rub her ass like it was a magic lamp. But I only needed one wish. India didn't budge.

OK, I thought, *now if I can just slide my index finger under her thong*. At that moment India helped me by raising her left ass cheek up just a notch. Ten seconds later my fingers were so far inside of her, I was tickling her liver.

"Boy, what are you do—ooh," she moaned.

"I'm doing you, baby," I responded, then fucked India like she was on a conjugal visit.

"After that night, we dated for two years and were inseparable. I even took her home to Louisiana to meet Lucille Brown. That was a big deal because I had only done that with one other girl. My mother loved India. She treated India like the daughter that she never had. We were going down south every three or four months. India even went a couple of times without me. During the week, they talked on the phone so much I thought my mom was trying to mack her. She was crazy about that girl. Shit, I was crazy about that girl."

Dr. Carter stood and walked over to the window. He pulled out a stick of gum and stuck it in his mouth. "Interesting," he said, chewing slowly, savoring the minty taste. "You said you proposed?"

"I did."

"What happened?"

* * *

It was a warm Saturday in June. We had just watched a hilarious poetry performance in Central Park by a young Puerto Rican lady who compared PMS to chemotherapy. India was still laughing about it when I told her to close her eyes.

"India," I said, bending to one knee, "if I had one day left to live, I would spend half of it telling you how much I love you and the rest of it making love to you." She opened her eyes and started crying as I opened the ring box. "Will you marry me?" I asked, batting my eyes like a basset hound.

She paused for what seemed like a full minute.

"Umm . . . hello?" I playfully said.

"I . . . I can't, LeBaron," she finally said, holding back more tears.

"What?" I snorted.

"Calm down, sweetheart," she said, pulling me to my feet.

"Don't tell me to calm down," I screamed. "Why don't you want to marry me?"

"I'm just not ready, LeBaron," she said, stepping back nervously.

"Why not?"

"I need to pass the bar; I have to get my career started. And I know this is going to sound fucked up, but I was going to tell you that I'm, uh—"

"You're what?"

She cleared her throat and continued, "I'm moving to California."

"You're what? When did you? Huh? This makes no sense."

"I'm sorry, LeBaron, I love you, but I have to do this. If I don't, I'll hate myself and probably you too."

Deeply wounded, I said, "I'm feeling like I'm hating somebody right now."

"C'mon, baby," she said, touching my arm. I pushed her away and stormed off.

"Leighton, I left her standing there in Central Park, and I took the next train back to D.C. That's the last time I'd seen her, until last night at Eric's party. She hurt me really bad."

"That's understandable," Dr. Carter said.

"But"—LeBaron cut him off—after all those years, I still wanted her. It was hard, Dr. Carter, I was weak."

"That's OK, LeBaron, we're all weak, but those of us who are strong in spirit can easily overcome the weaknesses of the flesh."

LeBaron smiled; he loved the way Dr. Carter phrased his answers. "And, you were so right when you said a man has to control his sexual desires before he can control himself." He waited for a response, but Dr. Carter just nodded and kept listening. "For the first time in my life I thought about the consequences, and, I tell you, I feel as if the veil has been lifted. But you know the killa thing about it?"

Dr. Carter grinned. "No, tell me the killa thing about it."

"I didn't decide not to have sex with this woman because I'm in love with Phoenix. Subconsciously, I think I couldn't stand treating another woman like a sex object. Besides, I've made a big mistake like that before, and it's something that I promised myself I would never do again."

"Interesting, tell me about this big mistake."

"Oh, let's see it was my senior year in college, and her name was Stacey."

I was straightening the ladies' pants rack at my part-time job at Shoe-town sports apparel store when I made up my mind that I wanted Stacey. She was walking past the store with a group of her coworkers from the K&B Drugstore next door. Her brown Levi's hugged her hips and thighs like a diver's wet suit.

Stacey was gorgeous, with a creamy caramel complexion, but she was a little ghetto fabulous. She always wore long acrylic nails, big-ass gold earrings, Tommy Hilfiger jeans, and fresh K-Swiss sneakers. We'd make quite a match, sorta like *The Cosby Show* meets *Good Times*.

I couldn't stop thinking about her as I stocked shoes, so on my lunch break I went next door and summoned the courage to ask her for a date. I was too nervous to be serious, so I thought I'd break the ice with one of my patented, yet stupid, lines.

I walked up to her and said, " I wish that I could change the alphabet."

She looked me up and down and smacked her gum. "Why?" she said.

With a silly grin on my face I said, "'Cause I'd put U and I together." She laughed. After she stopped laughing I asked for her number and if she would like to go out. She said yes. We fucked that night.

We lay in her bed afterward listening to R. Kelly's "Bump N' Grind." Her face was on my chest when I heard her sniffling.

"You got a cold?" I said, hoping that I didn't catch it. She raised her head to look at me. Her eyes were red, and tears dropped from her lids. "Why are you crying?"

" 'Cause I got a man," she said and lay her head back on my chest.

"Damn, you didn't tell me you had a boyfriend."

She looked at me once again and wiped her face with the back of her hand. Smiling, she said, "I don't, silly, I'm talking about you."

Aw, shit, was all that I could think. She had a boyfriend, and I had a fatal attraction. But she was dynamite in bed and cooked breakfast for me next morning, so it was all good. Damn, Stacey could scramble some eggs. I had never had a woman other than my mother and grandmother cook for me, so I was hooked. Besides, I was in college, and a good meal was hard to come by. Even though Stacey hadn't cooked me any spaghetti, I was beginning to think that she had put roots on me.

We dated for nine months before I cheated on her. I slipped bad. She caught me kissing a girl from school in the parking lot in front of Shoe-town when she was driving by with her chicken-head friend Michele. Stacey broke up with me that night. I was devastated. Yes, she caught me cheating, and I was the one who was hurt. Ain't that some shit? No one had ever actually said they didn't want to ever see me anymore. That hurt. I couldn't eat or sleep. I even dedicated a song to her on the *Quiet Storm*. I can still hear the DJ now, "This one is going out to Boopy from LeBaron. Girl, give that boy one mo' chance."

I called every damn day and when she'd answer she'd hang up. After we split up she got a new job at the Wal-Mart across town. One day I called there to ask her if I could pick her up.

"Sure," she said, "I get off at nine."

I was there at 8:30. I waited. Soon it was nine and no Stacey. 9:10, no Stacey. At 9:20 I went in and asked the customer service lady to page her and she said, "Stacey is off tonight." Damn, played again. I was fucked up in the head. I was so mad that I went home and ran two miles in slacks and church shoes. A few days later I ran into Michele at the K&B. I asked her how Stacey was doing.

"Just fine," she said as if she relished in sharing the news, "she has a new boyfriend named Tim Washington."

No! No! No! Tracey left me for Tim "Killer" Washington. A hardened criminal and convicted felon? I didn't want to believe it, but it was true. I don't know why, but

Michele also said that Tim drove a brown Toyota Celica. She shouldn't have told me that, because every time I saw a brown Celica I was looking in the window for Stacey. I didn't even know the car's year or model, so I damn near broke my neck trying to look inside brown Celicas for her ass.

I still kept trying to get back with her, and after about a month of begging and ass-kissing, Stacey finally agreed to go out with me. We went to the movies to see *CB4* with Chris Rock, then we went to Bennigan's. It was just like old times, me and my baby—I was so sprung. After we got to her apartment I got out of the car and followed her like I had done a million times before.

"Where are you going?" she snapped with an attitude.

"With you," I answered.

"I don't think so, LeBaron. I need some time to think about us," she said nonchalantly.

I said, "What? What's up? You have somebody else coming over?"

"No, it's just we're moving too fast; I'm still mad at you," she said.

"OK, that's fair," I said and left.

I floated back home, thinking that I was back in there. I had an 8 A.M. class the next morning, so I thought I'd bring her some flowers and put them at her door so she'd be surprised when she left for work. I picked up some flowers at a twenty-four-hour grocery store on the way to school, and when I pulled up in front of her house what did I see but a brown Toyota Celica. The windows had dew on them, so it had to have been there all night. I was stunned, crushed, and on the verge of suffocating. I called her on my cell phone. I managed to control my breathing as I dialed her digits. "Hello, Stacey," I calmly spoke.

"LeBaron?" she groggily answered. "Why are you calling me so early?"

I ignored that. "You sleep all right?"

"Yeah," she said.

"By yourself?" I countered.

"Of course," she said in that vague voice you use when you don't want the person next to you to know what you are saying.

"Stop lying, bitch!" I screamed like a lil bitch. "I see Tim's fucking car outside your damn apartment." She slammed the phone into the cradle. Right then, I understood how O.J. Simpson felt.

I drove to class in a daze and wasn't looking forward to two hours of biology. I didn't hear a word the professor said that morning. I couldn't get that car out of my mind. After class was over I declared the rest of the day a holiday just for me. I needed time to plan a way to get revenge on Stacey. I went into Victor Newman mode.

As I got in my truck to go home and plot, I couldn't stop thinking about her betrayal. I had to find out how she could do some shit like that. My hands shook as I dialed her number. On the third ring Tim answered the phone. "What?" he said, like it was his phone.

Now I was pissed. Stacey had never let me answer her phone. I went blank; I had no idea what I was going to say. Then suddenly I said, "I'm LeBaron. I know Stacey told you about me."

"Yeah, so what you want?" he said in his best Ice Cube impersonation.

"We need to talk," I told him. I had no idea what we were supposed to talk about, but I had opened the floodgates.

"About what?" he said.

"Uh . . . there are some things I need to tell you about Stacey that you need to know about," I said. Damn, I was really going out like a bitch.

He said, "Go 'head."

I said, "No, not on the phone, in person."

"Well," he hesitated, "it'll have to wait until I finish eating my pancakes."

Finish his pancakes? I felt like the Road Runner had dropped an anvil on me. She cooked that nigga homemade pancakes? I lost it. Stacey had never made me any fucking homemade pancakes! Eggs yes, but pancakes? This was personal now. Then I heard a lot of laughter in the background. She was laughing at me, along with some other people too. I was out there, at some Texaco station, sick with jealousy, making an ass out of myself, and that bitch was having brunch with a bunch of felons?

I started to call the cops. I was sure Tim had some dope on him or was about to plan a bank robbery or something else illicit. I was trippin' hard. I said, as calm and controlled as a lunatic could, "Okay, meet me at the Texaco on the corner in twenty minutes." He hung up. I looked at the phone and said, "Fuck you too."

So there I was, sitting in my truck thinking of ways to kill Tim and Stacey. I fantasized about breaking the door down with an axe. I bet that would've scared their asses. Tim would be shitting them pancakes and Stacey would be cowering and begging for mercy. I'd walk over to her and chop one of her damn legs off! Then I'd take it with me and throw it away. The way I figured it, I might've gone to jail, but I would've eventually gotten out. But every time she looked at that stump she'd say, "Damn, I shouldn't have fucked over LeBaron." I fantasized a few more minutes before I decided against that scenario. I was too scared to go to jail.

After thirty minutes had passed, the dreaded raggedy-assed brown Toyota Celica pulled up with two guys in it. "What a piece of fucking junk," I thought. "This nigga ain't no killa, he's Lamont Sanford." However, I didn't count on Tim bringing a friend. He must have thought that I was going to jump him, or, worse yet, he was planning to jump me. I strolled up to the car, eyeing Suge and Tupac, trying to figure out which one was Tim. Was he the passenger? A slim, brown skinned, rat-looking nigga? Nah, he didn't look like a killer, he looked like a killer's rat-looking sidekick. It had to be the driver, who looked like a black-assed Tim Washington. At that moment I was thinking the strangest shit. Like why do more black folks than white folks have the last names of presidents? Anyway, my adrenaline was pumping, and I took the offensive by asking, "Which one of you is Tim?"

The driver said in a mousey voice, "I'm Tim." I thought, *This nigga didn't sound like a killer.*

"You wanna walk with me over here so we can talk?" I said.

He said, "Nah, whatever you have to say you can say it in front of my boy here."

"You don't want him to hear this, I promise you," I said, although I didn't even know what it was he wouldn't want his friend to hear.

He replied, "Man, say what you got to say."

In my best J.R. Ewing impersonation, I said, "If you and Stacey had sex, I hope you used a condom." He and his boy had perplexed looks on their faces.

He said, "Nigga, what the fuck you talking about?"

Aw shit, I made him mad, I thought. But I braced myself for my ace in the hole. I looked at the ground, shrugged my shoulders, and in a solemn voice said, "Bruh, it's too late for me. . . . I just hope it ain't too late for you."

I saw the shock in his partner's eyes and the panic in Tim's. Tim spoke in a small, panicked voice that I'm sure he was used to hearing from his victims.

"Huh? HIV?"

I ignored it and once again said, "It's too late for

me. . . . I just hope it ain't too late for you." And then I walked away and got into my car. His raggedy-ass brown Celica didn't move. I said to myself as I drove off, "Think about that shit next time you're eating your fucking pancakes."

"Damn, I could have won an Oscar for that performance, or I could have gotten killed over that stupid shit too, but I didn't care, I was crazy. Another case of sex on the brain. You told me at the beginning of our sessions that things don't just happen. If I wouldn't have been looking at her ass, maybe I would have seen what my libido wouldn't let me see."

"And what is that, LeBaron?" Dr. Carter said.

"That we weren't even compatible. It's crazy how a brother can disregard the obvious just because a woman is pretty or has a nice body. If we did we could avoid a lot of trouble. And in retrospect, I can't be mad at Stacey. I was the one who cheated first. And you know something else? I never even apologized."

"LeBaron, I'm impressed. You have made great progress in our sessions. What else have you learned?"

"Well, I've learned a lot of things. First, before I love my woman, I must first love myself. Before, when Eric and I were running the streets, I didn't really love myself. Yeah, I loved the clothes, the clubs, the coochie, but I didn't love me. If I did I wouldn't have disrespected myself, the women I supposedly loved, or wasted my time on all that unimportant bullshit. Another thing I've learned is that there is more to a woman than her body. I feel stupid that I've wasted so many years chasing sex. I never even knew most of the women I supposedly loved. Didn't know their favorite colors and flowers. Hell, I didn't know all of their last names. But Dr. Carter, the most important thing that I have learned is that I love Phoenix for all the right reasons. It's time for a wife, a family, a beautiful house, and a dog."

"Are you sure you are ready for that now, LeBaron?" Dr. Carter smiled, barely hiding the pride he felt for his patient.

LeBaron didn't hesitate or think before the words fell from his mouth. "I am."

"I agree, that's why this is our last session."

"What? Why?" LeBaron's question sounded more like a plea.

"Because you're ready. The rest is up to you now. The next time that I see you will be at your wedding. Say hello to Phoenix for me."

LeBaron stood up to shake Dr. Carter's hand but instead hugged him. "Thanks, Leighton."

"No, LeBaron, thank you."

"One last thing?"

"Yes, LeBaron."

"Well, I've been the one doing all the talking. I thought that maybe you'd be doing all the explaining."

Dr. Carter looked LeBaron in the eyes. This time the green eyes didn't make LeBaron nervous. "The answers are always in here," he said, pointing his finger at his head. "Most of the time, we just need to hear ourselves say what the problem is."

Chapter Twenty-two

Without traffic, Tiffany's was a fifteen-minute drive from Dr. Carter's office. LeBaron made it there in less than ten. He had no time to spare, because the store closed at six and it was nearly five forty-five. After parking in the lot across the street, he ignored a red light and jaywalked, narrowly missing the oncoming cars. The same white security guard that had sneered at him the first time he and Eric had been there was at the door.

"We're closed," the guard said.

"C'mon, man, it's only quarter to six."

"Doesn't matter. I said we're closed."

John Van Dyke witnessed the exchange from behind the counter and walked over. "Hello, Mr. Brown, what seems to be the problem?" He remembered LeBaron because he had seen him several times over the past two weeks.

"Your doorman here says you're closed."

"Nonsense, we have fifteen minutes left. Please, come in." LeBaron gave the doorman a smirk and walked past him. "How may we help you today, sir?" Van Dyke said.

"I know this may be odd, but I want to exchange the earrings back for the ring I bought."

"You want the ring back? Change of heart, Mr. Brown?"

"You could say that, but I promise you this time the sale will be final."

After exchanging the earrings, LeBaron put it inside his jacket pocket and left the store floating. Phoenix was due back in two days and he would be at the airport to meet her, this time to ask her to marry him. He detached his cell phone from his belt clip and decided to call Eric and tell him the news. This time there would be no talking him out of it. The crossing light on Wisconsin Avenue turned red, and the road was clear. Dialing Eric's number on his cell phone, and consumed with thoughts of how he would propose to Phoenix, LeBaron started across the street.

"Hey! Watch out!" the guard from Tiffany's yelled, but it was too late.

The taxicab making an illegal U-turn swerved to the left, but LeBaron's legs wouldn't move. The force of the car threw him nearly twenty feet into the street.

LeBaron saw Phoenix's smiling face in front of him, and he didn't feel any pain as he hit the ground. While slowly fading into unconsciousness, he thought it ironic that out of all the times he'd tried to flag a cab down in that part of town, this was the first time that one had stopped.

Chapter Twenty-three

"By far, the best line this year has been Chanel," Maxine said as she and Phoenix walked through the hotel lobby. "And, judging by how my ass feels, it was the longest." Phoenix didn't respond or laugh at Maxine's wit. "Are you all right, dahling?" Maxine said, concern splashed across her face.

"Huh? Oh . . . yeah why?"

"You've been distant today, like your mind is in another place."

It was true, Phoenix felt odd. She couldn't put her finger on it, but she felt that something was wrong. "I'm fine, just a little worn out."

"I bet that Chance is an animal, right?"

"I wouldn't know." Phoenix shrugged off Maxine's question.

"What? Don't tell me you two haven't—"

195

"We didn't."

"That LeBaron must still have a hold on you. You young girls today."

"Yeah, but also I just met Chance, and I don't really know him."

"What? The man's gorgeous, he's built like a temple, and he's rich. What else is there to know, dahling?"

"You're crazy, Max."

"I'm crazy, but I'm happy." They laughed as they walked past the registration desk. The young clerk waved. They waved back, but he kept waving for them to come to the desk. "Excuse me, Mademoiselle Morgan," he said, "you've had quite a few messages."

"Really, how many?"

"About ten."

"Ten?" Phoenix and Maxine said in unison. "From who?" Flipping through the messages, the clerk said, "They all seem to be from a Bridgitte, she said she's a friend of yours." Phoenix turned to Maxine.

"That's my girlfriend, something must have happened." She turned back to the clerk. "I need to borrow a phone."

"Yes, mademoiselle, please come this way."

The clerk ushered Phoenix and Maxine to a private office behind the concierge's desk.

"Thank you," Phoenix said, choking back her anxiety.

"It's going to be all right, dahling." Maxine put her arms around Phoenix's shoulders. Phoenix's hand shook as she dialed Bridgitte's cell phone number. It seemed like forever, but within two rings she answered. "Bridgitte, this is Phoenix. I got all of your messages. What's wrong?"

"LeBaron was hit by a car."

"Oh my God!" Phoenix wailed. "What happened?"

"He was crossing the street or something and a cab hit him."

"Is he OK?" Phoenix braced herself .

"I don't know. He's hurt bad, Phoenix."

"No! No! Where is he?" Phoenix sobbed. "Where is he, Bridgitte?"

"He's in intensive care at GW."

"Oh God! Oh God no! Is anybody there? Where's Eric?"

"He's there, girl. He called me to find you. And a few people from the station are there."

"Is his mother there?"

"No, not yet, Eric called her, she's flying in."

"What did the doctors say?"

"They don't know, Phoenix. All I know is it's real bad. You better come home."

"I'll catch the next flight out."

"I'll pick you up at the airport."

"I'll call you back when I know the flight and time." Bridgitte hung up, and Phoenix handed the phone to the clerk and burst into tears.

"Phoenix, what happened?"

Her chest heaving, Phoenix fell into Maxine's arms. "It's LeBaron . . . he's been hurt . . . hit by a car."

Maxine gasped. "Will he be all right?"

"I . . . I . . . don't know. They say it's bad. I've got to get home, Max."

"Don't worry about it. Go upstairs and pack. I'll take care of the arrangements."

Maxine handed Phoenix a lace handkerchief, and Phoenix hugged her like she was family. She ran to the elevator patting at her tear-stained face. When the car came, she pressed the button for her floor and rode upstairs in uneasy solitude.

Phoenix turned to the only one who could save LeBaron.

"God, please let him live. I want him . . . I need him . . . I love him. There's so much I need to say to him. So much I want to do with him. I want to have his children. Our family is at stake, God. If he doesn't make it, I don't know what I'm going to do. Please, God, just let him pull through. I never had a last chance to tell him that I love him. I didn't even say good-bye."

Chapter Twenty-four

Eric hated hospitals. He hated the coldness, the smell, but more than that, he hated what hospitals symbolized. For a ball player, a trip to the hospital could mean the end of a career, and Eric's had ended in this very hospital. But today he hated the hospital because it was where his best friend was fighting for his life. LeBaron's prognosis wasn't good. He had a punctured lung, internal bleeding, two broken ribs, and a broken arm. The doctors said his chances were fifty-fifty at best. Eric had been in the waiting room of the ICU for nearly six hours while they'd operated on him. Since LeBaron's mother hadn't arrived yet, he was the first person allowed to visit him. Eric's heart sank as he walked into the private room.

"You can only stay for a few minutes," the nurse said. "He's heavily sedated and won't even know you're here."

"Thanks," Eric said, sitting down in the big wingback

chair next to the bed. He winced at the sight of his best friend with tubes and wires attached to him.

"I know you can hear me, LB. It's me, your main man Eric. I came as soon as I heard, and nigga you know how I feel about hospitals? I called your momma and she's coming tomorrow. She's fine—worried, but fine. Phoenix's on her way back from Paris too, Bridgitte told her what happened. That girl loves you, bruh. Y'all need to go 'head and get married when you get better."

The various monitors hooked up to LeBaron blipped in the background. Eric searched LeBaron's sedated face for any sign that he could hear him. Finding none, he continued. "One thing 'bout hospitals, man, they got some fine-ass nurses in here. I was trying to holler at one earlier, you should have seen her, dog. She looked like Halle Berry and had more ass than a donkey. Dig this crazy shit, though. I follow her, right? And she goes around the corner into this room. Some kind of treatment room that had all these beds and curtains and sick people all around and shit. So she went behind this one curtain. You know me, I figure I'll wait and holler at her when she came out.

"But, dude, guess what? I hear her strapping on some gloves or something, then she tells this old dude behind the curtain, 'Sir, you'll feel a little discomfort.' The old dude says, 'Hey, hold on! What you doing, young lady?' Then she goes, 'It'll be OK, sir,' and before he could fight her off I hear him groan like she was shoving a snow shovel up his ass. So she says, 'Sir, you have some bad hemorrhoids

there, but you'll be fine if you take four of these supposito-
ries a day for three days.' And get this shit, the old dude,
who by now is out of breath says, 'I got to stick that in my
ass again? Oh hell no! Ain't you got some pills or cream?'
She says, 'No, sir, we don't.' Then he says, 'Well, my ass is
just gon' have to hurt. Where I'm from men don't be sticking nothing up our ass.' Behind the curtain, I concurred.
Then she walks out from behind the curtain and there I am
standing right there. She looks at me and says, 'Hello, sir,
go behind that curtain and take your pants off, I'll be right
back.' Shit, you know I said fuck that and got the hell outta
there. I must have missed the sign that said Ass-digging
Room above the door."

Eric laughed hard at his joke. He thought he could
detect a grin on LeBaron's face through the haze of drugs.

"Sir," another nurse said, coming into the room, "you
have to leave now. We have to do some tests."

"OK, one second." Eric turned and whispered into
LeBaron's ear. "I love you, man, you gon' pull through
this." He then looked up at the ceiling and prayed, "God, if
you save him, I promise to settle down." If Eric had looked
back as he walked out the door, he would have seen
LeBaron's lips curling into a slight smile.

Chapter Twenty-five

The nurse's station in the Intensive Care Unit at George Washington Hospital was eerily quiet. It was nearly midnight, and most of the day's trauma and drama had left with the dayshift. There were only two people working on the floor, both of them black—one at the far end buffing an already spotless floor, and the other at the station buffing and filing her long nails.

"Go ahead, girl, I'll be in there," Bridgitte said, motioning to the waiting room. "I know you want to go in by yourself."

Phoenix nodded and kept walking to the nurse's station. She seemed dazed and hadn't said ten words since Bridgitte had picked her up at the airport.

"Hello," Phoenix said to the nurse.

"Visiting hours are over," the nurse said curtly.

Phoenix restrained herself from knocking the nail file

out of the nurse's hand. "I understand, but this is a special case."

The nurse rolled her eyes. "They're all special cases, ma'am."

Phoenix took a deep breath. "My boyfriend was in a bad accident, and I just flew in all the way from Paris and I need to see him."

"Paris, really?" the nurse said. "Why didn't you say so?" The nurse paused for dramatic effect, then continued. "In that case you can see him ... Um ... Let me see ... tomorrow morning at nine. That's when visiting hours resume."

Phoenix reached over the desk, swiped the metal nail file from the nurse's hand, and pointed it between the nurse's fake blue eyes. "Look, bitch, my boyfriend is in critical condition. I just flew ten fucking hours and if you don't let me see him, I will kick your black ass before you can call security."

"What did you say his name was?"

"LeBaron Brown," Phoenix said through gritted teeth.

"Yes, ma'am, he's right down the hall in Room 3322. You can only go in for a little while, and if he wakes up don't let him talk."

Phoenix dropped the file on the desk. "Thank you," she said. *Bitch*, she thought.

"You're welcome, and I'm sorry. I didn't—"

"It's OK." Phoenix turned on her heels and walked to the room. She steeled herself before pushing the door open. LeBaron's room was full of flowers, teddy bears, and get-well cards. There was even a copy of *Black-Tail* with a red ribbon tied around it, courtesy of Eric. The sight of LeBaron lying there shook her.

"My poor baby," she whispered. She put her bag down on a tray table and knocked over a cup of water.

"Oh, shit," she said, bending down to pick it up. When she stood up, LeBaron was looking at her.

"Oh God!" She jumped back. "I'm so sorry, baby, I didn't mean to wake you."

LeBaron swallowed hard and, although barely audible, managed to say, "I . . . missed . . . you . . ."

"Don't talk, sweetheart. I missed you too. I'm so sorry about the night at the restaurant."

He shook his head and tried to speak, but the words refused to come out. His throat ached from the breathing tube.

"Please, don't talk, LeBaron, the nurse said you shouldn't talk." He pointed at the pen and tablet on the nightstand. "You want the tablet?" He nodded. She brought it over, along with the tray table for him to write on. As he struggled to write, Phoenix couldn't help but stare at him and think of how handsome LeBaron was. The man looked good even in critical condition. Done writing, he handed the tablet to her. He had scribbled *I love you* on it in big ugly letters.

"Oh, baby," she said, wiping fresh tears from her cheeks, "I love you too."

LeBaron's outstretched hand begged for the tablet back. He turned the page and began writing again. When he was done, he pointed again at the nightstand. "The nightstand?" she said. He shook his head and pointed lower to the first drawer. "Oh, the drawer? You want me to open it?" LeBaron nodded, and Phoenix opened the drawer. Her heart stopped when she saw the small box from Tiffany's. She had a flashback of the last time she'd opened a Tiffany's box and how it had turned out to be a Pandora's box. Confused, she looked at LeBaron for an explanation. He nodded his head again, and she reached in to retrieve the box. Slowly she opened it, not really knowing what to expect. When she saw the diamond ring, she looked at LeBaron in disbelief.

"Honey . . . baby . . . what?"

He held up the tablet, and on it was scribbled the words *Will you marry me?*

"Of course I will!" she screamed. "Yes! Of course I'll marry you!" In her excitement she hugged him tight and kissed him. Within seconds LeBaron began to cough and shake violently. The various monitors started blinking and making unusual sounds. Phoenix panicked. "Oh God! Oh God!" she screamed. Then the heart monitor LeBaron was hooked up to flatlined. It was a long, awful, dull sound. "No, God! No!" Phoenix said again and ran out of the room screaming. "Nurse . . . Nurse . . . Somebody help!"

Epilogue

It was a warm and sunny morning on the day LeBaron's friends came to send him off. Many of his boys hadn't been to church in years, but they wouldn't miss this for the world. They had to send their main man LB off right; they knew he'd do the same for them.

It was quite a turnout, too. The pews were getting crowded, many of the people already getting emotional as the men's choir sang softly in the background. As the latecomers walked through the big, heavy wooden doors of Mount Calvary Baptist Church, the guests marveled at all the flowers. The bouquets were a sea of vibrant shades of purple, LeBaron's favorite color, purple violets and roses dancing while beautiful displays of birds of paradise towered regally, like plant royalty. Outside, the sunshine reflected off the two long black limousines slowly pulling up in front of the church.

A few older women wiped tears from their cheeks as the cars came to a stop. They stopped and stared as the white-gloved driver walked around and opened the door. Phoenix stepped out of the car crying but looking magnificent in her long white Vera Wang wedding dress. It had been a gift from Maxine. "She looks like a fairy princess," a little black girl said to her friend. Phoenix felt like a princess walking into the church. But her eyes were on one person, and he was at the other end of the aisle.

LeBaron looked like a black James Bond in his traditional black-and-white Gucci tuxedo, and the ivory cane he leaned on added a certain sophisticated charm to the outfit. It had been six months since the accident, and he was almost fully recovered. With the exception of a few minor aches and pains, he was feeling better than ever. His physical therapist even said that he could get rid of the cane in a few weeks.

He smiled as his mother dabbed tears from her eyes. Finally, she was happy with his decision. A tear fell from LeBaron's eye as he watched his woman walk down the aisle. There was no doubt in his mind that he had made the right decision.

He looked deeply into Phoenix's eyes. His mind was in a daze for most of the ceremony, until she nudged him.

"Huh?" LeBaron said, clearing his throat. Everyone in the church laughed, including the minister, who happened to be Phoenix's grandfather.

"Well, do you?" the minister said.

"Uh, yes I do," LeBaron finally said.

"Then, by the powers that God has vested in me, I pronounce you man and wife. You may kiss the bride."

A few hours later, at the reception, the couple laughed as Eric got wide open on the dance floor. Earlier he'd done his best man duty and had given them a touching toast that had ended with, "May your love be forever in bloom like flowers in the spring." A short while later he managed to jump out of the way when LeBaron threw the garter.

"Not the kid!" he yelled.

"Say what? You must have forgotten the promise you made to God when I was in the hospital that you'd settle down," LeBaron said.

"Nah, bruh," Eric yelled over the sounds of Funkadelic's "One Nation Under a Groove." "I didn't say I'd settle down, I said I'd boogie down." Everyone laughed as he pimp-walked to the dance floor, then did the robot down the Soul Train line.

"Congratulations, LeBaron," a familiar voice spoke from behind.

Recognizing it immediately, LeBaron turned around, smiling. "Dr. Carter, I mean Leighton, thanks for coming."

"It is my pleasure."

Noticing the slender, attractive woman holding his hand, LeBaron playfully whispered, "Who is this lovely lady?"

"LeBaron, I'd like you to meet my beautiful wife, Tina."

LeBaron raised his eyebrows. "It is a pleasure to meet you, Tina."

"The pleasure's all mine." Tina turned to Phoenix and said, "My dear, you look marvelous."

"Thank you." Phoenix beamed.

While the women chatted, LeBaron pulled Dr. Carter to the side. "What happened to Angela?"

"You know, LeBaron, after our sessions I thought it was about time that I took a dose of my own medicine."

LeBaron gave Dr. Carter a pound. "That's great, Leighton. I wish you two luck."

"The same to you, my friend. Oh yeah, one other thing, I owe you one more session."

"One more session? But I thought we were done?"

"Remember when I told you of the importance of man and woman?"

"Yeah."

Dr. Carter smiled, looking at Phoenix. "Now I need to tell you about children."

"Um . . . you better mark that appointment in pencil."

Dr. Carter laughed out loud. "Good luck, LeBaron."

"Thanks, Leighton."

As Dr. Carter and his wife walked away, Phoenix asked, "How do you know that guy? He looks familiar."

"Oh, I think he's a psychiatrist or something. You probably saw him on TV," LeBaron said, wrapping Phoenix in his arms.

After a few hours of dancing, eating, and talking, the newlyweds were tired and ready to leave. They had to catch a flight to Hawaii for their honeymoon. Outside, Ali's limousine waited to take them to their new home to change clothes, then on to BWI Airport. LeBaron had wanted to go to Paris, but Phoenix had insisted they go to Hawaii. Ali tucked a bridesmaid's phone number into his pocket as he held the limo door open for the glowing couple.

Before LeBaron and Phoenix made it to the limo, Reverend Dr. William Morgan pulled LeBaron aside. "Young man, I want to wish you and my granddaughter all of God's blessings."

"Thank you, Reverend."

"Also, young man, I have a question. My wife and I are about to celebrate our fiftieth wedding anniversary."

"Fifty years? Congratulations, sir."

"Thank you, son. Well, see, I was thinking of getting her a new ring to renew our vows."

"OK, sir," LeBaron said, nodding his head.

"And I was wondering, that's quite a ring Phoenix has there. Her grandmother really likes it. I mean, she really likes it, son."

"OK?"

"That ring must have set you back a pretty penny, huh?"

"It did," LeBaron said, smiling.

"Well, if I wanted to buy a ring similar to that, what would I be looking at spending?"

LeBaron leaned in close. "Reverend," he whispered, "you'd be looking at around fifteen grand."

"Fifteen thousand dollars! Damn! Uh hum, excuse me, I mean darn. Did you say fifteen thousand dollars? Young man, you spent fifteen thousand dollars on a ring?"

"I sure did, Reverend," LeBaron said, squeezing Phoenix.

As the Reverend walked out of earshot, LeBaron hugged his new bride closely and whispered in her ear.

"You know something, baby? For me, it's not about how much the ring costs, it's what it represents."

"And what is that, sweetie?"

"It symbolizes the bond of love and trust that I share with you. It symbolizes my journey to find you. Because of this ring I was able to understand the meaning of true love. This ring helped me realize that you are the only woman I have ever loved."

Please enjoy the following excerpt

of Bryon Harmon's new novel,

coming soon from Pocket Books.

Eric Swift had always dreamed of making love to Janet Jackson and tonight his dream was about to come true. Actually, he was going to have dinner and drinks in her suite at the posh W Hotel on Lexington Avenue in Manhattan. Eric had tried, without success, to convince her to come to his apartment at Trump Place, a new luxury development on the Upper West Side. But Janet had said she was tired and wasn't up for the crowds of people who would definitely be out on such a hot Friday night.

He donned a beige three-button linen Prada suit, smiling at the way the light set off the mustard silk shirt. The tailored suit fit him like a glove, but as he looked over his outfit he frowned at his footwear.

No, no. he thought. *These just won't do, too old.*

He strolled over to his walk-in closet. It looked like a Men's Wearhouse showroom with all the racks of tailored suits and rows of shoes.

Eric scanned the neat boxes of shoes until his eyes rested on the perfect pair. *Yes, these babies will do.*

Eric was a freak for shoes but not just any brand. He only wore Mezlan's, an expensive brand that had to be ordered from Spain. He carefully slipped on the brand-new brown Mezlan Amalfi's and then the matching belt.

"Goddamn," he exclaimed at the mirror, impressed with his reflection.

"Mirror, mirror on the wall. Tell me, am I the flyest motherfucker of them all?" He paused, laughing at his rhyme. "You damn skippy," he said, turning to walk out of the bedroom.

He still couldn't believe how lucky he was. Who knew that his boy Andre would know a woman as fly as Janet Jackson? Kenneth Andre, better know to his pals as "Dirty Dre," wasn't known for his taste in pretty women. Not that he didn't have any women. In fact, he was quite a player. It's just that his teams wore ugly uniforms. "Ugly women need dick too," was his motto. It didn't matter if the club or party was full of blind, naked and horny Tyra Bankses, Dirty Dre would somehow manage to leave with Harriet Tubman. That's why Eric wanted proof when Dre told him about Janet a month ago.

"Nigga, you want proof?" Dre said, reaching into his back pocket for his wallet. "Here's your proof." Eric held the photograph up to the light and studied it. He was impressed.

"Well, I'll be damned, Dirty. How did you meet her?"

"She and my sister go way back. They did ballet or some shit together when they were little girls."

"Well, Miss Jackson ain't no little girl no mo'," Eric said, his hand on his crotch. "She looks old enough to control this."

Eric had called her later that week and they'd hit it off great. She was funny, charming, and above all, fine as hell. He couldn't wait to hook up with her.

Early evening traffic in Manhattan was always crazy, and Eric arrived at the W Hotel about twenty minutes late.

Fuck it, he thought. *I'm late, but I'm fashionably late plus I'm fly as a mutha-fucka.*

He was so excited he started humming the chorus to Michael Jackson's "Beat It" as he pushed the elevator button. And that's exactly what he planned to do to Janet. He couldn't believe how nasty she talked on the phone. His heart was racing by the time he knocked on her hotel door.

"Just a minute," Janet said.

"Oh, it's gonna' be more than just a minute," Eric muttered to himself. As Janet turned the lock, he stuck his right hand in his pants' pocket and cocked his chin a few degrees to the left, his most mackalicious pose. As the door swung open, Eric thought he heard trumpets blaring and angels singing. There Janet Jackson stood in all her glory, in a sexy white formfitting dress with a V-neck that dipped to her navel. Her feet, which barely peeked out from under her dress, were laced in a pair of three-inch heeled pink-and-white Jimmy Choo sandals. She wore a pink flower in her long black hair and on her neck and wrist were a matching platinum and diamond necklace and bracelet. She looked even better than her picture.

Eric had planned to say some smooth shit, but all he could spit out was "Goddamn!"

Janet's laugh was sweet. "Is that all you've got to say, Eric?"

"If I say what I'm thinking, you might call hotel security," he said shaking his head.

Janet smirked. "Go ahead. I'm sure I've heard it before."

Eric got down on one knee. "Will you marry me?"

"What? Boy, you are even crazier than Dre said."

"Look, I know a preacher who makes booty calls, I mean house calls. I got his two-way number and I can get him here right now."

"Your pastor has a two-way? Wait a second, what would we do for a ring?"

He pulled a ring off of his finger. "You can wear this."

"That's a graduation ring."

"It's gold."

"Boy, come on in here."

"I plan to."

Janet grinned and turned around slowly. Eric's eyes were watching her shapely ass in slow motion. One cheek, then the second, and as she began to walk, Eric blinked his eyes. Then he blinked again.

"What the fuck?" he mumbled.

Janet was limping. Not a simple sprained-ankle limp, but a full-blown she-must-have-had-polio-as-a-little-girl limp.

She looked over her shoulder. "Don't be scared, walk this way."

"I can't walk that way," Eric said, dazed and confused.

Janet looked surprised. "What's wrong? Didn't Dre tell you?"

"Tell me what?"

"That I have a prosthetic leg."

Eric swallowed hard, eyes bugging. "You got one leg?"

"Yeah, I had a traffic accident about five years ago and they had to amputate my left leg."

"Huh?" Eric stuttered. "You left your leg? I mean you lost your left leg?"

"I can't believe Andre didn't tell you."

"Motherfuck!" Eric said shaking his head.

"What did you say?"

"Oh, um I said you had some tough luck."

"It's okay, at least I'm alive."

"Yeah, that's one way of looking at it."

"So what now? You don't wanna come in?"

"Uhm, oh yeah, I'm cool."

Eric closed the door. It sounded like a cell door clanking on death row. He tugged at his shirt collar and cleared his throat. "You have anything to drink in here? I'm feeling a lil' parched."

"Yeah, I ordered a nice bottle of wine."

"What kind?"

"A Merlot."

Eric frowned.

"You don't like Merlot? I can order something else. What would you like?"

"Some Mad Dog 20/20."

* * *

"A one-legged Janet Jackson? Please don't tell me you hit it?" LeBaron whispered into the phone. LeBaron was Eric's best friend but looked like his brother—tall and handsome. The two friends had had plenty of good times when they'd worked together at the FOX television station in Washington, D.C. That was in the past because LeBaron had recently married his longtime girlfriend Phoenix.

"Did I hit it?" Eric laughed. "Nigga, not only did I hit it, I damn near ripped off her prosthetic leg," Eric said. He was on his cell phone downstairs at Le Bar Bat, a trendy Manhattan bar on West 57th Street. It was the first First Friday party at the club and even though it was only 6 P.M., the club was starting to fill up.

"You are out of control," LeBaron howled.

"Shit, her legs were out of control."

"Hold on, Eric. I got something wild to tell you."

"You had sex with a girl in a wheelchair?"

"No, fool. Phoenix is pregnant."

"Phoenix is what?"

"That's right, dog." LeBaron beamed. "My ass is 'bout to be a daddy."

"Yo' ass is 'bout to be broke." Eric laughed, curling his lips into a disapproving frown. "How many months?"

"Three."

"Three months!" Eric straightened up on the barstool. "But damn, y'all ain't been married but a month. Who's the daddy?"

They both laughed.

"You know we've been married for nearly six months."

Eric raised his bottle and loudly said, "Well, I guess congratulations are in order, Big Poppa." Two people at the other end of the bar frowned. Eric frowned back.

"Whoa, try and contain your enthusiasm," LeBaron said.

"Oh, c'mon bruh. You know I'm happy for you. It's just . . ." Eric mumbled while staring at his beer.

"Just what?" LeBaron demanded.

"Why do you want to have some damn kids running around tearing shit up?"

"What?" LeBaron exclaimed in disbelief. "That may be the dumbest shit you've ever said."

"You know how I am."

"Yeah, petty."

"Whatever. First you get married, now you're having a baby. I mean, *damn*. We're the same age and shit. You're making a nigga feel old."

"You damn sho' don't act old."

"What's that supposed to mean?"

"Forget it, man."

"Yeah, later for that shit. We're supposed to be celebrating." Eric waved the attractive female bartender over. She could have been actress Gabrielle Union's younger sister.

"Listen to this, LeBaron," he said holding the phone to her ear. "Hey, Miss, can I get another round? My boy here is going to be a baby daddy."

"Well, congratulations," she said into the phone, "Your drinks are on the house."

"Well, fuck it. If it's free, I'll take a bottle of Cristal," Eric said, not believing his good fortune.

The bartender gave him a nigga-please look.

"Okay." Eric grinned. "Make that a Heineken."

The bartender was so cute and her smile was so perfect, Eric couldn't resist flirting. "Oh, my God, you have a beautiful smile." A devious grin spread across his face. "I bet when you smile, the sun gets jealous."

"Boy, you are crazy," she gushed. Her teeth were as white as Michael Jackson wanted to be. "But thank you. Yours is quite nice too."

"Thanks, I'm a dentist." Eric grinned.

"Really?" she asked.

"No," he said, laughing. "But you know something? You look familiar."

"Really?"

"Yeah, you look like my first wife."

"Oh, you were married?" she said arching her right eyebrow.

"Not yet." Eric deadpanned.

On the other end of the line, LeBaron nearly fell out of his chair laughing. He'd heard Eric use that line a thousand times and it killed him every time. The bartender didn't get it and walked off with a confused look on her face.

"You're still the same old Eric," LeBaron said. "Anyway bruh, how is the Big Apple treating you?"

"I'll tell you something, LeBaron. I thought that moving here was going to be fucked up, but I love it. I am in my element."

"We all miss you. It's not the same without you here."

"I miss you guys too, but you know everybody has to move on. You're on a whole other level with Phoenix now. You don't need me there to be fucking up a good thing."

"That's bullshit, E. You didn't leave because of me."

"I know." Eric laughed. "You don't need any help fucking up a good thing."

"Whatever. By the way, how's CBS? I heard they work a brother like a slave—"

Eric cut him off. "What TV station doesn't? But for five hundred fifty thousand a year, nigga I'll pick cotton on live TV."

"Damn." LeBaron laughed. "That's what they're paying you?"

"In large bills. Oh, and wait until I send you a tape of one of my co-anchors. Oh, my God . . ."

"What's her name?"

". . . the ass on her . . ."

"Eric, what's her name?"

"Her ass left me shocked and awed."

LeBaron laughed. "What's her name?"

"Oh, Eden."

"Eden?"

"Yeah, Eden Alexander. Isn't that a great name?"

"She cute?"

"Is she cute? Nigga, Webster's hasn't listed the word to describe what she is."

"Damn, she's like that?"

"She *is* like that. Nigga, she's hot as a firecracker," he paused, looking around. Then he lowered his voice to a whisper. "You know I got to get up in that."